THE BOY & THE BEAST

MAMORU HOSODA

YEN ON

NEW YORK

THE BOY AND THE BEAST
MAMORU HOSODA

Translation by Sawa Matsueda Savage

THE BOY AND THE BEAST
© Mamoru Hosoda 2015
©2015 THE BOY AND THE BEAST FILM PARTNERS
All rights reserved.
First published in Japan in 2015 by KADOKAWA CORPORATION, Tokyo
English translation rights arranged with KADOKAWA CORPORATION, Tokyo, through Tuttle-Mori Agency, Inc., Tokyo.

English translation © 2016 by Hachette Book Group, Inc.

Yen On
Hachette Book Group
1290 Avenue of the Americas
New York, NY 10104
www.hachettebookgroup.com
www.yenpress.com

Yen On is an imprint of Hachette Book Group, Inc.
The Yen On name and logo are trademarks of Hachette Book Group, Inc.

The publisher is not responsible for websites (or their content) that are not owned by the publisher.

First Yen On edition: February 2016

Library of Congress Cataloging-in-Publication Data

Names: Hosoda, Mamoru, 1967– author | Savage, Sawa Matsueda, translator.
Title: The boy and the beast / Mamoru Hosoda ;
[translation by Sawa Matsueda Savage].
Other titles: Bakemono no ko. English
Description: First Yen ON edition. | New York, NY : Yen ON, 2016.
Identifiers: LCCN 2015040344 | ISBN 9780316270601
Classification: LCC PL871.O88 B3513 2016 | DDC 895.63/6—dc23 LC
record available at http://lccn.loc.gov/2015040344

10 9 8 7 6 5 4 3 2 1

RRD-C

Printed in the United States of America

MAMORU HOSODA

PROLOGUE

"You really are a hopeless lot, you know that? You wanna know about him that much, eh? Sure, we know him *real* well. But look at you all, coming here with your mouths half open like roasted chickens, waiting to be fed information. It isn't the kind of thing we can tell you just like that. Look, to us, he's special. He isn't just any other guy—he's on a completely different level. Why should we have to share our precious memories of him with a bunch of fresh-faced brats showing up at our door? Beat it. Didn't you hear me? I said, get outta here."

"Don't make such a fuss about it, Tatara. Why not tell them the story? They, too, think he's special—it's not just us. His name is spoken even in the most isolated of locales nowadays. These lads came all the way to this hermitage hoping to hear about him, didn't they? You know that no one else can tell his story in as much detail as you can—besides myself, that is."

"Still, y'know?"

"It's good of you all to come. Now don't be shy. Come on in."

"Hey now, Hyakushubo."

"Well then, do you all drink loose leaf tea?"

"Wha—?"

"You do now, do you? Well, that's just fine. One, two, three, four, five, six, seven, eight... So, Tatara. You'll tell these youngsters about him, won't you?"

"You've got to be kidding me."

"No need to be nervous. Tatara here might sound like he's annoyed, but he's actually bursting to tell the story to someone. That's the reason this hermitage never lacks for visitors. Here's the tea. It's hot. Go on, pass it around to the ones in the back."

"…Hey, you lot. Don't tell me you're just gonna stand around while you sip the tea. Aw, what the hell."

"What did I tell you?"

"Space is tight in here, so sit close together in a circle. Come on, people. Well then, as a special privilege, we're gonna tell you the story, all right? So clear out your ears real well and listen up. …Oh, and Hyakushubo, some tea for me, too."

"Of course."

"Once upon a time, but not that far in the past, mind you… Just a wee while ago."

"Of the countless cities of beasts in the world, nowhere is as lively as it is here in Jutengai. The cone-shaped valley, eroded by a murky, iron-rich river of reddish brown, is home to roughly one hundred and three thousand beasts today. For many years, a grandmaster watched over these beasts, but one day out of the blue, he declared that he would retire and ascend into godhood."

"They say that there are eight million gods, and as you know there really are a ton of gods in this world. The gods bless the life and death of every little thing. Not just of beasts but of the sky, the oceans, the clouds, the mountains, animals, plants—even down to each roadside flower and every tiny little bug. If that isn't enough, they even watch mercifully over those ugly creatures they call 'humans.' Goes to show just how honorable they are. Each of those gods is a former beast that reincarnated into godhood. You might say beasts are smack in the middle between everything worldly and the gods. But not all beasts can become gods. How could they? I mean, look at the lot of you. Not one of your faces looks fit to become a god, even if heaven and earth got flipped somehow, am I right? Only the particularly virtuous among us beasts rise to greatness and can be reborn as gods."

"The grandmaster was named Ugetsu, and he was a peaceful man with a perpetual smile who had the appearance of a snow-white rabbit with long catfish whiskers. He was also said to be the greatest martial arts master since the dawn of Jutengai. Yet here he proclaimed that old age was forcing him to leave his post. 'While I contemplate what kind of god I shall become, you must all prepare to choose a new grandmaster,' he said."

"Now that put the city in an uproar. The grandmaster's imminent retirement was a shock beyond measure. Sure, many lamented this loss or were reluctant to say good-bye, but at the same time, every single beast was happy for the grandmaster's ascent to godhood. But then the beasts all wondered: Who would become the next grandmaster of Jutengai, when that post eventually opened up? Who most deserved to take on the role?"

"The one to succeed the position had to display the utmost strength, dignity, and moral conduct.

"In beast society, convention defined beasts to be 'warriors serving the gods,' and the traditional wisdom was that warriors naturally had to excel in martial arts. That's why one of the foremost qualities required in a grandmaster was 'strength.' In any beast city, you're bound to see a certain number of warriors wielding their various weapons, but Jutengai was particular in that muscle alone wasn't enough to demand respect. Rather, what one needed was true strength backed by mental toughness, the kind that incorporates courage, leadership, and high esteem. Next came 'dignity.' I shouldn't even have to bring up the grandmaster as an example. It goes without saying that whoever it was needed the grace and stature worthy of representing all of the people in Jutengai. Finally, 'moral conduct.' A stable disposition was obviously ideal for representing the city. Who then, of the hundred thousand beasts, fit that criteria?"

"An immediate candidate was a boar beast named Iozen. Calm and collected, courageous and bold, he was a respected man with a ton of apprentices. Not only was he a listed member of the city council, he also oversaw the martial arts institution The Jutengai Guard. He was also a father to two sons, Ichirohiko and Jiromaru. He was a prime candidate, no doubt about it. Everyone supposed he'd be the next grandmaster. At least, that was the word on the street."

"There was another beast who was considered a possible candidate. Named Kumatetsu, he was covered in shaggy hair like a bear. With a seemingly bottomless supply of stamina, he would scamper around like a monkey, swinging his prized great sword around every which way. He had the build worthy of a warrior, and many agreed that in terms of brute strength, he surpassed even Iozen."

"But the guy wasn't without his problems. Everyone acknowledged his strength, but he was also a rude, arrogant, self-centered brute, so he didn't have a single apprentice."

"And how, I ask, could a man like that ever hope to have a son?"

"That's when the hero of our story came from beyond the world of beasts—that is to say, from the world of the *humans*."

"Have any of you ever gone to the human world? I assume most of you haven't. Although the worlds of beasts and humans are distinct and separate, the two worlds actually resonate in some ways. The human world has made astonishing physical developments, but the underlying systems, technologies, and designs supporting those developments were often passed on from beast to human. For example, most of the assorted human ideas and concepts about the gods were originally propagated from our notions and history.

"On the other hand, sometimes things that have little use in our world made unique developments in the human world. One of those is 'writing.' You know how our world values ideas but tends to eschew writing for having little use? Just like a wise man once said, 'I cannot see why living knowledge should be recorded by a lifeless medium such as writing—pictures are more befitting the attempt.' But go to the human world, and you will find it filled with writing, writing, writing on anything and everything. That bizarre sight of writing all over the city makes me shudder. It almost makes me question whether humans actually want writing to rule their lives."

"Just goes to show how completely different our world is from the human world. That's why..."

"Yes."

"See, if we're gonna tell this story, there's a bunch of things in it about the humans that we can't express properly in our words—that's the problem."

"So..."

"So. From here on out, we'll be telling it in his words."

"That is to say, we shall tell it as if we are him, from his perspective."

"What's that? We're nothing like him? He doesn't have an old monkey face like mine? Shut your mouth, you little squirt."

"Ha-ha. You will have to excuse my scrawny pig's snout as well, for the time being. Not to worry, though. Keep listening, and in this candle-light, our ragged faces will soon seem to take on the valiant features of our hero's face.

"Now then, are you ready?

"Let us begin..."

REN

The summer after I turned nine, I was all alone.

The city of Shibuya at night reeled in the awful humidity. Bright images flashed nonstop on the huge screen of the QFRONT building, and a succession of large trailer trucks emitting deafening music passed by. Every time the light changed, a surprisingly huge crowd of people jostled to scramble through the intersection. Everyone was dressed up, and everyone was laughing as their heels clicked against the pavement.

There I stood, in the middle of the intersection. The neck of my T-shirt stretched out. Hair a messy clump. Skin grimy, gone for days without washing. My body thin for want of a decent meal. A plastic convenience store bag dangling from my hand.

I glared sharply at the faces of the people passing by, looking so happy, so oblivious, so carefree.

I was just a brat with no place to go, cast aside from the world.

Across the way, I saw some tough-looking policemen with a secure hold on a couple of young girls, dragging them along by their arms to the police box in front of the station.

"Come along, now."

"Stop touching me."

"You kids ran away from home, didn't you?"

"Did not."

"I can tell a lie when I hear one, okay?"

I slipped into the crowd to avoid being spotted by the policemen, hurried over to the other side before the light turned red, and passed through the entrance to Center Gai Street. Dome-shaped surveillance cameras set up all along the street peered down, determined to catch anyone looking suspicious. I glared back at each and every one of them as I disappeared off to a place beyond the cameras' stares.

One backstreet away from the bustling main road, there were suddenly no pedestrians in sight. The cold light of a vending machine illuminated the alleyway and its contents. Storage compartments entirely covered in graffiti. Pipes stretching from the buildings. Outdoor air-conditioner condensing units. Some cardboard boxes stacked awkwardly on top of one another. A standing ashtray filled with cigarette butts. It was a break area for those workers out on the main street who were calling out to potential customers. No one was there at the moment. Apparently, they were all too busy to even take a break.

I leaned back against one of the storage compartment doors and slumped onto the ground.

I broke off a bit of bread from inside my plastic bag and tossed it into my mouth. The bread was completely dry, having been out of its bag for days, and made a stiff crunch when I bit into it. This was all the food I had at the moment. All the money I had in the world was a few 10,000-yen bills and some loose change in the pocket of my shorts. I did a mental count of how much I had left as I chewed sparingly on the bread.

Then—

"Squeak…"

Hearing a soft, trembling noise made by some creature, I jerked my head up to take a look. But all I saw were some empty cans littering the asphalt that had fallen from an overflowing recycle bin.

"……?"

"…Squeak."

Two tiny eyes peered out from behind an empty can.

A mouse? No. This was much smaller, with long, fluffy white fur. It wasn't like any creature I had ever seen before, and it was staring intently at me... Well, not at me, exactly. It was looking at the parched piece of bread that I was eating.

"Okay, hold on."

I tore a bit off and held it out on the palm of my hand in front of the tiny thing. Startled, it shrunk back behind the empty can. I gently placed the piece of bread on the ground and pulled my hand away.

"Go on. Eat up."

Despite my offer, the little creature didn't move, looking back and forth between the bread and me for a while. But eventually it came out from behind the can and started on the bread. Faint crunching noises came from its tiny little mouth.

"...Did you run away from somewhere, too?" I asked without expecting an answer.

The diminutive thing simply lifted its tiny eyes up toward me and blinked.

I was all alone.

A bunch of adults I didn't know came into the apartment that belonged to my mom and me.

They proceeded to pack everything in our home into cardboard boxes with practiced efficiency. Boxes sealed with packaging tape were rapidly stacked into piles. My mom's clothes, her shoes, her bed— everything was being carried out the door.

"We should get going, Ren."

My uncle called my name, sliding his suit sleeve up to look at his watch. This uncle and the other relatives from the head family were the ones directing the moving company to carry out their task. I didn't answer, hugging my knees to my chest with my head down in a corner of the room near the windows.

"Um, what shall we do with this?" one of the movers asked hesitantly.

I heard an aunt from the head family saying, "Oh, we'll take care of that ourselves." I looked up. On the dining table was an incense holder with a single strand of smoke wafting up from the stick it held. Next to it sat a small urn containing some ashes and a picture frame bearing my mom's face from when she was still alive.

I kept staring at that face.

My uncle opened his mouth. "Ren, I realize you might be sad that your mother is gone all of a sudden, but it was a traffic accident. There's nothing to be done. The head family will take you in and be your legal guardians now. Do you understand?"

"You're the only boy in the family, and the precious future head of our house. We'll make sure you want for nothing, now that we'll be raising you."

I thought about what my aunt meant by "want for nothing." I had heard once that it was a wealthy household with lots of real estate in the city. But I had hardly even talked to these people before.

I caught a glimpse of my dad's face in a photo that had slipped out of an album. Back when we were living in a much smaller apartment, my mom, dad, and I had bunched up together to take that picture. Times were fun back then. I had been much smaller, and more importantly, the three of us had all been living together as a family. I had no idea back then what would become of me in the future.

"Ren! Speak up if you heard me!" my uncle said, raising his voice.

I distinctly remembered another time I had heard him yell like that. He had suddenly showed up at our apartment with a lawyer and forced my parents to separate. It probably had something to do with the fact that I was "the only boy in the family, and the precious future head of the house." My mom cried through it all. It was always that way. These people used the same tone of voice whenever they forced something to go their way.

But my dad was the one who infuriated me, much more than the relatives from the head family. Why didn't he do anything when my mom was crying? Why did he accept what those people told him to do?

"Why isn't my dad here?" I asked my uncle.

"Forget about him."

"Why? My dad's my dad."

The aunt interjected. "You know that he and your mother are divorced now, don't you? The court granted custody to our side. He's just a stranger now."

"Then I'll live on my own from now on."

"Don't be ridiculous. How could a child like you do that?" My uncle scoffed through his nose.

I glared as hard as I could at that nose.

"I will too live on my own. I'll grow big and strong and get back at you all!"

"How dare you speak to us that way? Ren, you—"

"I hate you. You, Dad... I hate you all!"

I burst out the door without waiting to hear the rest.

Night was falling again on Shibuya.

I had to find somewhere to rest before it got too late. Somewhere with a roof, where I could get by without anyone finding me. But that night, some spots were already occupied, some were under construction, and some were taken over by people having some fun. I was having trouble finding a place that worked. I had been walking for so long that my legs and body both felt heavy.

Along the way, I saw countless kids in the arms of their parents. Every time I did, I felt something tingle in my chest. The faces on the kids clinging to their parents looked so happy, so oblivious, so carefree. A voice echoed from inside my chest.

I hate you.

Something indescribable was raging inside.

I hate you... I hate you...

Whatever it was wanted to get out of my chest. It was beating against the door so hard that it was ready to break through. I forced myself to push it back down. But the harder I tried to push, the stronger it seemed to beat back.

I hate you… I hate you… I hate you…

That's when I realized. This was a curse. A curse on those awful relatives from the head family. A curse on my dad who wouldn't come help me. A curse on every happy, oblivious, carefree thing—everything other than myself.

I hate you… Hate… Hate… Hate…

The curse shot up violently from deep within my chest, over and over again. I couldn't stand the choking feeling anymore. I felt like I would burst if I didn't spit it out.

In that moment, a tremendous force swelled up, and the curse was finally unleashed:

"I HATE YOU!"

I found myself yelling the words out loud.

The grown-ups around me stopped in surprise. All eyes turned on me, wondering what had happened. I couldn't bear it and turned my back on them. One of them even approached me, asking, "What's wrong?" with a kindly face and a hand extended toward me. I pushed the hand aside and started running to get away.

And so I ran, leaving behind the thing that had been raging inside me a moment ago.

A train rattled loudly as it passed overhead.

In a bicycle lot beneath some elevated tracks, I sat amid a cluttered row of parked bicycles and buried my face in my folded arms. I had no choice but to spend the night there. I was so incredibly tired that I didn't even have the strength to look up.

Chiko poked its head out from under my shirt. This was the tiny creature I had found in the back alley of Center Gai. I named it Chiko for the word that means "tiny." Chiko rubbed its fluffy fur against my forehead, squeaking as if to comfort me.

"Squeak. Squeak."

"Chiko, I'm fine. Thanks."

Chiko continued squeaking worriedly.

"Squeak. Squeak."

"I'm fine. I'm a little tired, though, so just let me sleep..."

"...Sque—"

Suddenly, Chiko stopped squeaking and burrowed quickly into my hair.

I could hear some people talking as they approached.

"...Geez, what do they want from me? If I'm stronger than Iozen, what more do I need? Dignity? What the heck is that?"

"That's a pretty tall order from the grandmaster, if you ask me. Remember how long your last apprentice lasted?"

"A month... A week? ...No, a day..."

"It was a morning. A morning!"

Two men trod by in front of me with their sandals flapping on the pavement. One spoke rapidly in a high-pitched voice, and I figured he must be relatively small. The other had a deep voice, probably a burly man. The second man boisterously spit out his frustration.

"I just can't stand the kinds of wusses who cry, okay?!"

"You think you can afford to be choosy? You might as well pick a human or scrubbing brush or something off the street and make *that* your apprentice."

"Bah, fine. Then I will!"

The burly man suddenly turned on his heel and came back my way. I sensed the smaller man's alarm.

"Hey, I was kidding. Don't take it seriously!"

The sound of the burly man's footsteps approached and stopped suddenly in front of me.

"Oi."

"......"

I kept my head down and didn't answer.

"I said, *oi*."

The burly man slammed his foot down in obvious irritation.

Why are you talking to me? Leave me alone.

The man went on in an incredulous tone.

"You dead or alive, kid?"

"...Go away."

"If you can talk, then you're alive. Where's your mama?"

"Go away." Don't ask me about my mom.

"Your old man, then?"

"Shut up." Don't ask me about my dad.

"Answer me. Your old man, where—"

"Shut up, shut up, shut up, shut up!" Unable to take any more, I lifted my face and shouted. "If you keep talking, I'll kill you!"

Both men were wrapped from head to toe in long, hooded cloaks. The burly man had some kind of long, stick-like object in a bag on his back. It was dark inside their hoods, obscuring their faces. But there was no hiding the distinct smell that filled the air. The type of smell that one might find, for example, standing before an animal enclosure at the zoo...

"Kill him? A brat like you?" scoffed the smaller man.

"Quite the feisty one, eh? Let me see your face properly."

The burly man slowly stretched his arm out from under his cloak and abruptly grabbed my chin, forcing it up.

That was when I first saw the face deep inside his hood.

Sharp fangs peered out from inside a bearded mouth.

The nose protruded outward like a bear's.

And the eyes looking down at me were those of a wild animal.

"......!"

I was completely paralyzed with shock.

"A...a beast...!"

I couldn't believe what I was seeing.

The burly man stared down at me without moving. His eyes were more intensely red than anything I had ever seen in my life. I felt like those eyes saw straight through everything in my chest, sizing me up. Paralyzed, all I could do was let out a petrified moan.

"Aagh..."

The moment of assessment ended abruptly.

Thrust away by the burly man, I slammed onto the ground.

"Ow!"

"Not bad," he said in a satisfied tone.

"Come on, that's enough."

At the smaller one's urging, the burly man turned his back on me.

However, he stopped after a few steps to turn back and spoke to me once more.

"You. Wanna come with me?"

"……?!"

My heart emitted a sharp thump at his words.

"Wha—? Don't be stupid, Kumatetsu!"

The smaller man rushed back and started dragging his burly companion away.

I came out from between the bicycles and looked after them in a daze.

I saw the two cloaked figures go out from under the tracks and up the stairs leading to the west exit of the station. What had I just seen? A dream? A hallucination? Some kind of joke? Or maybe…

I found myself running after the two of them, hoping to find out.

The lights changed, and a crowd of people started walking all at once.

I sprang into the middle of the busy intersection and looked for any sign of the burly man.

There was the neon sign of the Sanzenri Drugstore, flashing blue. QFRONT. The gate to Center Gai Street. The 109 building. Shibuya Mark City. The JR Shibuya Station…

I looked all around but didn't see the cloaks anywhere. All I could see was the bustling square, no different from usual. I rubbed my eyes fiercely.

"What was that just now…? Was it a dream, after all?"

Then suddenly, someone grabbed my arm firmly from behind.

"?!"

I whirled around in surprise. I thought it must have been that burly man.

But it wasn't.

"Hey, kid, did you run away from home?"

Looking down at me was a young, tough-looking policeman.

"You know, a kid shouldn't be out alone at night in a place like this."

Another policeman, this one bespectacled and middle-aged, peered down at me beside the first. It was the team of officers who had caught the two runaway girls earlier.

"Don't you know that's against regulations?"

"L-let me go."

I twisted my body in an attempt to escape. But the young policeman had such a powerful grip on me that I couldn't move, no matter how much I struggled. The middle-aged officer took a clipboard out from under his arm and started asking questions.

"What elementary school do you go to? How do we contact your legal guardians? We'll have them come get you."

I snapped my head up to look at them. My uncle and aunt from the head family popped into my head. Were those people my legal guardians now? *You've got to be kidding. I'd rather die than go with them.*

"No… No way… No!"

I pried myself out of the policeman's grip and ran into the sea of people.

"Get back here!"

"Stop!"

I ran blindly through the intersection and into the crowd on Center Gai Street.

The policemen pursued me at a terrifying speed. But the mass of pedestrians blocked their way, seeming to deter them.

Meanwhile, I turned into this alleyway and that in an attempt to throw them off. I could no longer see the policemen behind me. Still, I ran on without stopping. I couldn't risk getting caught. No way was I going to the head family. They weren't my guardians. I didn't have any guardians.

Then…

All of a sudden, I glimpsed the cloaked figure from earlier out of the corner of my eye.

"?!"

I jerked to a stop.

I saw the back of a hulking figure slip sideways into a narrow opening, between some buildings in a far corner of Center Gai.

It was definitely that burly man from before.

But as soon as I blinked, the cloaked figure had disappeared completely. There was no one in the narrow opening. All I could see was an air-conditioner condensing unit, an exhaust vent, a bunch of pipes, and a store's trash can.

"......??"

I was bewildered. I was sure he had been there just a moment ago...

Then I heard the policemen's voices.

"Where did he go?"

"This way, maybe?"

I could see them searching for me, leaning up to peer over the ocean of people.

I looked in turn at the policemen and then at the narrow opening where the burly man had disappeared. I also mentally compared my relatives from the head family with the beast I had seen.

That gruff voice I couldn't get out of my head echoed once more in my ears.

You. Wanna come with me?

My heart pounded. It wasn't as if I had anywhere to go to begin with.

I would much rather deal with a beast than live "wanting for nothing" with those relatives.

I had made up my mind.

With big, determined steps, I started toward that narrow gap between the buildings.

KUMATETSU

The narrow opening led into a strange passageway.

A hazy green light illuminated the uneven cobblestones and bumpy clay walls. The narrow passage was only as wide as both of my arms spread out to either side, and more of the same seemed to stretch on and on. The farther I went, the more confusing the passages became. Every so often, I would find a bamboo basket of flowers placed on the cobblestones, as if to mark the spot. I used them as markers to go on but soon came to a dead end. I doubled back, following the map I had drawn in my mind, but the flowers that should have been there were now gone. Wondering if I had missed a turn, I used a pot of flowers dangling from the wall as my next marker. But when I returned once more, I couldn't see those flowers anywhere.

It was like a maze.

But that wasn't all. In the wall of the passageway was a window. No frame or aluminum sashes, just a hole in the wall. A gray-haired cat sat in that opening, staring this way without moving an inch. In another window, a rooster with an impressive tail at least two meters in length had its head turned this way, cocked to one side. In yet another window, a little potted tree with flowered branches sat on its own. A look beyond the window, however, revealed a Japanese deer with antlers shaped like those branches, observing me intently.

A deer?

"I-is this really Shibuya……?"

The words fell out of my mouth as I backed away.

I sensed movement behind me and turned to see the shadows of some figures pass by in the light reflected off a distant wall much farther in. From their sizes, I figured it must be the two cloaks. I hastily ran in that direction and turned the corner. But the figures were already turning another corner in the distance. I ran once more to get closer. But every time, the figures were far off at the end of the passage. No matter how much I ran, I couldn't seem to catch up. How could that be, when they were just walking?

I came to a crossroads, where I suddenly lost sight of the two of them. Though I scanned the passages stretching front, left, and right, all that was there was a vase of flowers sitting on a stool in each direction. It was a dead end. Not a soul was in sight.

"Huh…? Huh…?"

Not knowing which way to go, I was rooted to the spot.

It was then that Chiko poked out of my shirt and squeaked as if to warn me. The steady rhythm of hoofbeats on cobblestone approached from behind. I turned around and opened my mouth in shock.

It was a horse.

The long face of a horse was closing in on me.

"Aaaahh!"

There was no space to run in the narrow passageway, and I was helpless as the horse pushed me along with its nose. The passage that had been a dead end just a moment ago suddenly seemed to open up. I could sense a wide-open space with a bustling crowd of people drawing near. The horse, which carried many sheets of textiles on its back, was headed straight in that direction. There was nothing I could do but keep on yelling.

"Aaaaaargh!"

The horse pushed me out of the passageway, and consequently, I hit my head on the cobblestones with considerable force.

"Ow. Uggh…"

The horse that had been pushing me stood up on its two legs, with the huge load of cloth still on its back, and gave me a questioning stare as it strode by.

Two legs?

I snapped my head up in surprise.

The place was a large stone manor of some kind and, under its tented courtyard, was a large gathering of strange-looking men bustling about, lit by the honey-colored glow of some lamps.

The overpowering smell of wild animal hit me. All of the men had the faces of animals.

An impressively antlered cashmere goat was discussing a deal with yarn in hand. An alpaca spread open one of the fabrics he sold. Some camels stretched their necks forward to evaluate the goods. An angora goat negotiated prices with a notebook in one hand while counting on the other. Rapidly counting bills was a llama with expert manipulation. Courier horses shouldered the bundles of textiles already accounted for and carried them out.

Oh no.

They were beasts. This was a town overrun by beasts.

On the verge of tears from fear and anxiety, I found myself screaming before I knew it.

"Aaah!"

My voice caught the attention of the goat in the middle of discussing his deal. The sheep all turned my way one by one. From all over, I felt the beasts concentrating their eyes on me.

No. Oh no.

Sensing danger, Chiko flew back into my shirt. I hastily stood up and turned to rush back into the passage where I had come from. But somehow a wall stood where the passage should have been.

"Huh…? Huh…?! The way I just came through is gone!"

How? When? Why? No matter how hard I looked, there was no passageway there—only a plastered wall barring my path. Cold sweat erupted all over my body.

The beasts murmured as they all gave me looks mixed with surprise, suspicion, and curiosity.

No, no, no.

I needed to run, anywhere as long as it was away from there. As soon as I started running, I tripped over my legs and fell on all fours. *Damn it.* Undeterred, I remained on all fours and forced my arms and legs forward to escape as fast as I could.

"The exit… Where's the exit…?!"

The main street in the town of beasts was lined with numerous stores and filled to the brim with festive energy. Large cloth banners were hung above the street in multiple layers, glowing with wicked shades of blue and red and purple that I had never seen before. Beasts enjoying the town at night flooded the street, and I ducked lower to hide myself as I zipped through on all fours. After a while, I saw a large gate at the end of the street and the circular blue neon sign affixed to it, flashing regularly. Red neon lights in the center framed the yellow characters displayed there.

JUTENGAI.

That was what it said. From what I could tell, that was what the town was called. On either side were the characters SANZENKAI and ROASTED CHESTNUTS, respectively. Its design felt familiar somehow, but what it was I couldn't remember. Passing through the gate took me out into an open square lined with cobblestones. Gentle hills curved up to the east and west from the square, and their slopes were packed with lights belonging to what looked like homes. The hills formed a valley where the square was. The square was apparently the heart of the city, and it glowed with exceptional brightness. The light came from the countless stalls set up there in rows. Pushed along by the sea of beasts, I shot into the teeming market of stalls.

Whole ducks, their skins crisp from roasting, hung next to stewed chickens with their heads still attached. Dried salmon showed off their ferocious teeth. A dried stingray glared like some grotesque alien. Pots overflowed with dried squid, starfish, frogs, lizards, and other unidentifiable items. Mountains of grains and fruits waited to be weighed out and sold. Bottles of alcohol were piled high. There were endless rows of pans, kettles, and earthenware pots. Accessories made from bones and shells of all sizes. A sword blade giving off a hellish glint, various fighting gear… Everything in sight was completely foreign from the world I had just come from. Attacked with a brutal feeling of isolation, I felt like I would be crushed by my anxiety at any moment. I had to find an "exit" quickly and escape this place. I had to get back to Shibuya. I chanted these words silently in my mind as I scurried the best I could on all fours.

"Huh?!"

All of a sudden, someone pulled on the neck of my shirt. With no chance to resist, I was lifted like a kitten. My captor was a thuggish wolf beast carrying a broadsword.

"…The heck is this?"

"It's a human kid."

"A human? What's it doing here?"

Two of his wolf buddies came up and peered at me with astonishment as I thrashed my limbs. This was in front of a stall selling Japanese instruments, and the three of them grabbed hold of some flutes, *biwa* plectra, and taiko drumsticks to pull on my cheeks and push up my eyelids.

"L-let me go!"

Ignoring my yells, the three of them brought their heads in together, grinned, and started a horrifying discussion.

"This is perfect. Shall we skin him to sell to the lute maker?"

"How 'bout we dry him up and shave him into flakes?"

"Or what if…"

I don't want to be like those chickens and salmon in the stalls! I couldn't stand it any longer and found myself screaming.

"H-help!"

Just then—

"Stop that, you fools!"

A sharp voice rang out in an admonishing tone.

The voice came from a scrawny-looking pig beast. Bald-headed with unshaven stubble, his black monk's robe was mottled here and there with what looked like moth-eaten holes.

"You mustn't say such sinful things."

He blinked his small eyes slowly as he reprimanded the trio.

Out of the corner of my eye, I watched the wolves grumbling in a huddle as we gradually left them behind.

Led by the beast in monk's robes, I made my way down a street lined with stalls.

"Now, don't take it to heart. Those fellows just have somewhat foul mouths and faces. There's no need to be afraid."

Despite what he said, I couldn't stop my body from shaking. The shrill laughter and yells of drunken beasts echoed ceaselessly from the midnight stalls. The beast in monk's robes spoke in a calm and gentle tone, probably to reassure me.

"My name is Hyakushubo. I'm an ascetic, as you can see. This is Jutengai, a place that can only be reached by taking the correct paths to get here. You see, we beasts, who have the potential to become gods, and you humans, who cannot, live in completely separate worlds. You must feel so lost, having accidently wandered in here like this. Come, let me take you back to your own world."

I hadn't expected this. Not all beasts were necessarily frightening. I supposed that some beasts were willing to help me out. I noticed that I had stopped shaking. In any case, it looked like this beast in monk's robes, Hyakushubo, would show me the exit, so all I had to do was follow him to get back—

"Hey, now! You really came, eh?"

I heard that loud, gruff voice I remembered from before.

I turned around to look and stared in disbelief.

The burly beast from earlier was thumping over this way, a grin filling his entire face. Instead of a cloak, he now wore a bright red jacket, with a crimson great sword on his back that was as long as he was tall. Some white hair peeked out from around his neckline. With his bear-like face, I guessed this beast was supposed to be a moon bear.

"Yep, just like I figured. I'm impressed, kid!"

Drinking gourd in hand, he stuck his red drunken face forward in high spirits and grabbed my shoulder, pulling me toward him with a yank.

"Kumatetsu, what are you doing?" Hyakushubo asked reproachfully, forcing me back toward him. "He's a lost boy. Treat him with compassion."

The bear beast called Kumatetsu twisted the side of his mouth in resentment. "Compassion, you say? You monks really say the wimpiest things."

"I meant don't treat him roughly."

"What's wrong with being rough? He's no lost boy."

So saying, Kumatetsu plopped his large hand on my head. "From this moment on, this kid's my apprentice!"

"...Apprentice?"

What? I never agreed to that.

"I told you so already. Did you forget?"

No, you didn't. How would I forget?

Hyakushubo cried out in astonishment.

"You're making a human child your apprentice?!"

"A human, a scrubbing brush, whatever. I say he's my apprentice, and that's that!"

Kumatetsu seized my head and shoved it back and forth.

"Wait, wait, wait."

Rushing in our direction was a monkey-faced beast. He looked like a craftsman of some kind, with an indigo-dyed jacket and cloth around his neck, and had a metal-clasped pouch rammed into the sash tied at his waist. Judging from his voice, this was the smaller man who had been with Kumatetsu before.

"I told him it was a bad idea."

"Tatara, tell me what led to this."

"The grandmaster insisted that Kumatetsu take on an apprentice if Kumatetsu was thinking about pursuing the responsibilities of grandmaster. That may be no challenge for Iozen, but no one's gonna want to be an apprentice to the likes of this guy. Heh. Then we were taking a gander at the wretched humans when we found this kid here."

Hyakushubo turned toward Kumatetsu in exasperation.

"So you abducted him?"

"He's the one who followed us."

"Still, you shouldn't drag him into something he has nothing to do with."

"You're saying I can't take an interest in a promising-looking kid? Is that it?!" Kumatetsu bellowed angrily.

Yet both Tatara and Hyakushubo seemed completely unfazed.

What kind of relationship do the three of them have? I wondered.

"After that, Kumatetsu muttered, 'We're going,' with his breath reeking of alcohol, and dragged the boy away, ignoring our objections. From the edge of the square, we watched the boy's little figure walking alongside Kumatetsu as they made their way up the slope next to the water tower.

"'How senseless can he be? Does he want to fill the post when it opens up that badly?'

"Hyakushubo furrowed his brow all serious-like, and I couldn't help but burst out laughing.

"'Nah, Kumatetsu just wants to win his fight against Iozen. That's all there is to it.'

"'True. I doubt he has any interest in becoming a grandmaster and eventually ascending to godhood.'

"'Even if he were to reincarnate, the best he could be is a god of some object or other—a *tsukumogami*. Like god of the toilet or god of the scrub brush.'

"'Will it be all right leaving a human child with Kumatetsu?'" Hyakushubo asked worriedly.

"'Who knows? It's not my problem.'"

"Personally, I wondered why he even gave a hoot about what happened to some human brat."

I went up the hill, chasing Kumatetsu from behind.

The main road branched off into narrower and narrower paths, and we proceeded to climb a huge number of steps. We gradually went from the bustle of town to a lonelier area with more noticeable litter on the street and graffiti on the walls. It felt somewhat unsafe and was clearly not an area where the well-to-do would ever live.

Kumatetsu's house was at the very top of the stone steps.

About the size of a one-bedroom apartment, it was perhaps better described as a "hut," with the paint peeling off of the concrete walls due to age. Weeds grew with wild abandon from between the tiles in the front yard, and a wire for hanging laundry swung in the wind on the roof.

Kumatetsu lifted the cloth curtain in the entrance facing the front yard and went inside. *Why a cloth curtain? What kind of house has no door?* I hesitated for a while, not knowing what to do. A feeble light turned on inside the hut. I realized that there was another entryway with a door. Apparently that was the main entrance. With no other choice, I braced myself and opened the front door.

The inside of the hut was so cluttered that it was hardly different from a garbage dump. Numerous articles of clothing hung haphazardly from a wire stretched from one wall to the other. Dishes were strewn on the table. Chairs were left lying on their sides. In a corner of the room was a tattered frame with KUMATETSU-AN—possibly the name of his dojo—written in it, propped up against the wall like an oversized piece of rubbish.

Kumatetsu kicked aside a random array of liquor bottles and shoes and half-eaten honey jars littered all over the carpet and threw a couple of small cushions down in their place.

"Sleep here."

"What do you mean 'apprentice'?"

"I'm saying I'll keep ya fed from now on."

"I never asked for that."

"Hmph. Whatever, then."

Kumatetsu sat himself down on the only extravagant thing in the hut—a large sofa with elegant trimmings. It was more a chaise longue than a sofa, the kind with fine leather upholstery that an aristocrat might take a midday nap on. It hardly fit in with the rest of the coarse hut and seemed utterly out of place. Kumatetsu scratched his belly noisily as he continued.

"I hate hearing wusses cry, though. Sob once, and you're outta here."

"I'm not gonna cry."

"That's what I want to hear."

"But that doesn't mean I'll be your apprentice."

"Then why did ya come with me?"

"Why…?" The words stuck in my throat.

"You don't hafta tell me. It's obvious. You ain't got nowhere else to go."

"…You're pitying me, then?"

"You blockhead. Save the tough-guy act for when you're a proper man!" Kumatetsu bellowed, then turned to the side and muttered as if to himself, "Either way, you've got no choice but to live on your own."

His words felt strangely sincere and convincing. I was speechless.

"……"

"I never asked you yer name."

"…I'm not telling."

"What?"

"It's personal information."

You shouldn't tell a stranger your name. It's important personal information. That was what my elementary school teacher told me. But it somehow felt absurd bringing up the concept of personal information with the bear beast before me.

"Geez. Then what about your age?" Kumatetsu bared his fangs in irritation.

Age was personal information, too. I hesitated, not knowing if I should tell him. But then I thought refusing him would only escalate this absurd feeling inside of me.

I held up as many fingers as I was old.

"Nine…?"

Seeing my fingers, Kumatetsu grinned as if he had thought of something, and leaned back into the sofa, satisfied.

"Heh. Then from here on out, you're 'Kyuta,' 'cause you're nine."

Kyuta? What kind of a name is that?!

"…Why should I let you give me a name?"

"Got that? It's 'Kyuta.' Well then, I'm gonna sleep now, Kyuta."

Without giving me time to protest, Kumatetsu rolled up in a blanket and turned his back on me.

What time was it now? Perhaps it was after midnight already.

I flipped the cloth aside and went out into the front yard. An astonishing number of stars twinkled in the sky, and down below, the lights of the bustling downtown area flickered. The cylindrical building that I had been informed was a water tower stood out distinctively. I was sure a similar cylindrical building stood at the bottom of Dogenzaka in Shibuya. Come to think of it, the building with the circular dome on top and the building with the series of ginkgo leaf patterns looked familiar as well. What could this mean? Did it mean that although this was a different world, it was somehow connected to Shibuya…?

"Ren."

A voice came from behind.

I turned around to find my mom.

She was standing outside the hut, wearing an apron with a tray in hand.

"I made omelet with ham. Your favorite. Let's eat before it gets cold."

My mom, who was supposed to be dead, was looking at me with a smile. I was losing track of what was real and what was a dream. But wasn't this city of beasts already like a dream anyway?

"Yeah. I'm coming," I called back to my mom. After so many recent surprises, I seemed to have gotten numb to any more. I started walking as if in a dream.

I took three steps, and my mom was already nowhere to be seen.

"......"

I felt like cruel reality had suddenly been thrust at me. Overwhelmed, I turned my back on the hut and crouched down to hug my legs. I was really, truly all alone. A hopeless sense of loneliness and sorrow pierced my entire body like needles. The tears were welling up. I desperately tried to force them back, but I couldn't stop the sobs from escaping my lips. Chiko poked out of my shirt and squeaked in a worried tone, then leaned on me as if to nuzzle. And yet the sobs came out one after another.

I hate hearing wusses cry.

Kumatetsu's words from earlier echoed in my ears.

Don't cry.

I told myself that over and over again.

Clang, clang, clang, clang!

A sudden loud noise made me leap awake.

"H-huh?!"

I looked to see Kumatetsu with a frying pan and a wooden mallet, smirking with his teeth showing.

"Time for grub."

The sky was blue and uplifting. It was morning already. Kumatetsu continued to slam the frying pan as hard as he could.

Clang, clang, clang, clang!

"S-stop that!"

I covered my ears and protested.

The night before, I had slumbered in the chicken coop at the bottom of the stairs. According to Kumatetsu, he had woken up to find me gone from the room and had thought I had run away. But then he found me sleeping in the chicken coop surrounded by the hens. I was confused, too. Why hadn't I run away?

Kumatetsu cracked raw egg after raw egg into bowls of rice.

"You still angry? C'mon, I was just having a bit of fun. Get over it and eat up."

Chiko was on my shoulder, nibbling on a pine nut. I alone refused to touch my food and said nothing.

"These eggs are fresh from the hens. It's a waste not to eat them raw."

The fresh eggs were still slightly warm from the hens' body temperatures. I had felt a warmth against my cheek as I slept in the chicken coop earlier and realized that it must have been from these eggs.

But I still refused to eat.

"Or aren't you hungry?" Kumatetsu asked, confused.

"Of course I am!" I yelled, unable to hide my resentment and hunger any longer.

"Then eat!"

"Not raw eggs, though!"

"Huh?"

"…They smell disgusting."

I loved food with egg, but I just couldn't stand them raw. I didn't get how people could enjoy the stuff.

"Who doesn't eat them? Watch."

I didn't get the bear in front of me, either. He slopped the egg and rice together in his bowl with chopsticks and shoveled all of it into his mouth at once then turned, his cheeks full of food at me and spoke.

"See?!"

I turned my face away from his stupid-looking expression.

"You look like an idiot."

"The hell you say?!"

A barrage of rice bits spewed out of the stupid bear's mouth, splattering all over me.

"Ack, gross!"

"Apprentices don't get to be picky!"

"I'm not your apprentice!"

"Shut up and eat!"

"No way!"

"If you're not gonna eat, no matter what..." The bear lowered his stance and readied himself.

"What are you gonna do?" I also lowered my stance, bracing myself.

"I'll throw it in your mouth!"

The stupid bear grabbed an egg out of the basket and came around toward me, but I sensed what was coming and dashed off almost simultaneously. Around the table we went, the stupid bear running after me like crazy and me running away as fast as I could.

Unbeknownst to us, Hyakushubo and Tatara had appeared at the window, peering in at me and the stupid bear going round and round.

"Stop that, Kumatetsu. Treat him gently."

"What did I tell ya, Kumatetsu? Now, get a move on and toss that annoying brat back where you found him."

Kumatetsu seemed deaf to both of these comments. I waited for an opportunity to escape the endless circling and went outside, then leaned in between the two onlookers and called out to the stupid bear running in circles by himself.

"I hate you!"

Finally realizing that I was gone, the stupid bear's face went red with anger, and he came after me.

"Get your ass back here, Kyuta!"

I went out of the gate and zoomed down the stone steps we had climbed the night before. *Kyuta? No way!* No way I was going to be his apprentice. The voice yelling far behind me faded off into the distance.

"Get back here, you! Kyuta!"

THE BATTLE FOR SUCCESSION

Jutengai during the day looked completely different from the night before.

As I made my getaway, I saw many beasts on their way to work. There was a peddler walking with a large load on his back, a vendor selling baskets on the go with countless baskets hanging off of a long bamboo pole, and a beast setting up scaffolding for some building repair. They were all working. I had to admit I had assumed differently. Despite being beasts, they didn't spend all their time fooling around every night, like in the old songs. (*What was up with that stupid bear, then? Sauntering about aimlessly with his sword on his shoulder, he was no different from a common thug.*)

To avoid suspicion, I pulled my T-shirt over my head to hide my face and looked for the manor with the courtyard from the night before. My guess was that I would find the passageway that could take me back to Shibuya there. It didn't take me long at all to find the main street with the hanging banners. In the sunlight, I saw that each of the colorful banners was made from different materials, with different dyeing techniques and transparencies. These were positioned in such a way to produce complex effects off of one another, like some kind of artistic experiment.

From the very beginning, I had thought this main street looked somewhat like Center Gai Street. The layout of the alleyways was almost exactly the same. But unlike Center Gai, which mainly featured shops, the backstreets here made up a workshop district where many artisans pursued their crafts. An indigo-dyer could be seen dipping raw thread into some liquid in a large pot, a weaver rhythmically working the loom, and a silkscreen printer applying dye to some fabric. All of their crafts had to do with cloth. There was also a fabric dealer bearing numerous rolls of fabric. I remembered that the courtyard in that manor from the night before had also seemed like a place to trade woolen textiles.

There were other types of workshops, too. One of them was a blacksmith's. I saw the smithies there working the red-hot steel, letting off great fiery sparks. Another blacksmith was hammering out a roughly formed piece of metal, constantly stopping to check its curvature. Its long, thin form was obviously that of a sword. I realized that these craftsmen were swordsmiths. I recalled that many of the beasts I had seen carried swords on their waists. The stupid bear did, too. Perhaps swords were of particular importance in this place.

I painstakingly walked through every alley, but I never did find the manor with the courtyard. I did see a whole lot of closed gates, so perhaps one of those had been what I was looking for. If that trading house was only open at night, there was no way for me to find it now. With nothing left to do, I went out into the square. The stalls during the day looked nothing like they did the night before. With some offering vegetables and other fresh produce, and some providing lunch items such as noodle soup, porridge, and pizza, the place was filled with the wholesome feel of normal day-to-day activity. A certain menacing trio had threatened to "dry me up and shave me into flakes," but seeing the place now made me think that perhaps they had been empty threats after all. Under the sunlight, the roasted birds and dried salmon that had seemed utterly grotesque the previous night looked simply delicious now. My stomach rumbled violently.

I spotted a couple of kids in front of one of the stalls, making my heart skip a beat.

Why were there kids here? But on second thought, it wasn't a surprise at all. Of course the beast world would have adults as well as kids, and parents as well as children. Judging from their heights, the two kids looked to be around my age. Their young faces didn't look particularly beastly or animallike, and looked barely different from those of human children. I concealed myself behind a stall selling winter melons and peered out at them, unnoticed.

I looked on as the one who was as roly-poly as a boar piglet was handed the fruit parfait he had ordered. It was a particularly tasty-looking parfait, with a generous pile of fruit cut into large slices.

"You want some, too, Big Brother?"

The other one, who was tall and slender, shook his head from side to side. Although apparently related, his pale, attractive face and calm demeanor made him a stark contrast to his brother.

"Okay. Then I'll eat it all myself." The younger brother plucked a piece of fruit off with his thick fingers. "First, an orange…"

An orange… I swallowed involuntarily.

"Ahhh."

Ahhh… My own mouth opened along with his. I hadn't had anything worth eating these past few days, and this morning in particular, I had stubbornly refused to have so much as a bite.

But the younger brother paused his hand. "I've changed my mind."

Whoops. I caught myself and hid behind the winter melons.

He then picked up a different piece of fruit.

"I'll start with a cherry instead. Ahhh."

Ahhh… I couldn't stop my mouth from opening along with his again. A streak of drool ran from the corner of my mouth and dripped down. I hadn't had anything worth eating these past few days and this morning in particular I had stubbornly refused to have so much as—

"Look, Jiromaru. It's Father."

Hearing his brother's cheerful voice, the younger brother stopped his hand again.

"Pops."

Whoops. I caught myself and hid behind the winter melons once more.

A beast with the face of a wild boar came and crouched before the brothers, placing his arms on their shoulders. He had a powerful body with a sword at his side, and a long snout with two large tusks. His golden hair and beard like a lion's mane made him look exceptionally strong, yet his face was gentle and smiling as he faced his sons.

"Ichirohiko, Jiromaru. Are you boys training hard?"

"Yes," the two brothers replied in unison.

The older brother who had been called Ichirohiko leaned forward.

"Father. Will you not take a look at my training?"

"Of course. Straightaway, even—"

The boar swordsman stopped short and glanced over his shoulder. Behind him was a group of large and formidable beasts like water buffaloes and rhinoceroses, all in an orderly line with matching jackets. An emblem of boar tusks was dyed onto their backs. Clearly, the boar swordsman was their leader. He turned back to face the brothers.

"I'll make some time, so will you wait a little longer?"

"What? Again?"

The younger brother, Jiromaru, seemed discontent.

But his older brother Ichirohiko gave his father a smile like a good boy. "Yes."

"I apologize." The boar swordsman stood up.

Suddenly, he seemed to notice something in the center of the square. "Kumatetsu!"

Kumatetsu?! I jerked my head around to see.

There he was in the lunchtime square packed with people, twisting his head around to look for me.

"Hey there, Iozen."

The boar swordsman called Iozen stepped forward to where Kumatetsu stood.

"So you finally got yourself an apprentice. At least, that's the word going around."

"Yep. But he ran off on me already. Have you seen him? He's a tiny tyke 'bout this high."

"A child? When you're pretty much a child yourself?" Iozen made a show of acting overly surprised.

"Aw, shut up."

Based on their interaction, I could tell these two knew each other quite well.

"Here's my advice as a father of two sons: Without the experience, you just don't have what it takes to look after a child."

"That so? Well, once I decide to do something, I don't change that for nothing. Anyway, I gotta find Kyuta. These human kids, I tell you. They're so damn fast."

Iozen, who had been relaxed up to that point, sucked in his breath sharply at those words.

"...A human? Wait, you're telling me that this apprentice is a human child?"

Just then—

"Master."

Having let down my guard, I had been caught by one of Iozen's water buffalo apprentices.

"Ow! Lemme go!"

The water buffalo had me by my hair and pulled me up high.

With legs thrashing in the air, I was the center of attention of all the beasts in the square.

"A human?"

"What is a human doing in our world?"

I could hear the brothers Ichirohiko and Jiromaru murmuring as well.

"A human. That's what one looks like..."

"Why's there a human here?"

"Ah, Kyuta!"

Kumatetsu shot me a smile that seemed to say, "Found you at last," but Iozen grabbed his shoulder to deter him, his voice strained.

"Hold it, Kumatetsu. I'm saying this for your sake. Take that child and leave him back where you found him."

"What's the big fuss over a human kid or two?"

The tension in Iozen's voice was heavy.

"You and most others may not know this, but there's a reason why we beasts live in a world separate from the humans. They say that in their fragility, humans harbor darkness deep within their hearts. If the darkness gets to them, and can no longer be controlled…"

"Darkness? Bah, I didn't see anything like that in him."

"Listen! This is a matter beyond just you."

"I decide what I do with my apprentice, y'hear?"

"Look, I'm warning you. Don't do this, for the sake of all the people in Jutengai!"

Iozen finally raised his voice threateningly. Beasts all around who had been enjoying their breaks stopped walking or leaned up to see what was going on.

Tensions were high now between Kumatetsu and Iozen as they faced off.

"For the sake of the people? Sounds like someone already fancies himself the new grandmaster, Iozen."

"What was that?"

"Then why don't you force me to stop? I wouldn't mind settling the matter of who takes over, right here and now."

With that statement, the square erupted in an uproar.

"It's a fight between Iozen and Kumatetsu!" somebody yelled.

"Finally!"

"Will this decide who the new grandmaster will be?"

The beasts withdrew at once to open up enough space.

At its center, the two slowly positioned themselves. Kumatetsu scowled at Iozen as he removed his red jacket with the sun emblem and tossed it on the ground.

"Kumatetsu! Calm down!" Hyakushubo shouted as he pushed his way through the crowd.

Meanwhile, Tatara egged him on irresponsibly.

"Yeah, yeah! Let's do this!"

The entire crowd of beasts was bursting with the desire to see the fight settled.

Off to the side, the three menaces from the night before had their heads together in hushed conversation.

"I say Iozen."

"I say Iozen, too."

"I say Iozen, too."

"Then what's the point in betting?"

Far from eager, Iozen let out a relenting sigh and grudgingly removed his jacket, handing it to Ichirohiko beside him.

Ichirohiko looked up at him with concern. "Father."

"Stay back."

Iozen untied the knot from his sash and pulled out his sword, scabbard and all, then put it in his right hand with the blade-side down and took a bow.

But Kumatetsu just kept twisting his body to stretch it out without bothering to bow back.

A murmur ran through the beasts at his attitude.

"What's Kumatetsu's problem?"

"Where's his respect?"

"Stretches?"

"Is he trying to be funny?"

"He should learn a thing or two from Iozen."

Ichirohiko was also infuriated at Kumatetsu.

"Observe the proper formalities!"

"As if he would have any regard for formalities."

Tatara seemed just fine, getting ready to enjoy the show.

Hyakushubo, on the other hand, seemed something of a worrywart.

"That idiot. He's made an enemy out of everyone here…"

Amid the storm of booing from the beasts, Kumatetsu whipped off his shirt to reveal his bare upper body and made a defiant expression. His manner was precisely the opposite of Iozen's, who had made a salute with his sword with his knees on the cobblestones before calmly tying the sword knot back onto his sash.

"Is it going to be a sword fight?" I asked Iozen's apprentice water buffalo, as I still dangled by my hair.

"The grandmaster has forbidden anyone to draw their sword."

The water buffalo was kind enough to show me the hand guard of his sword. "We all have our hand guards tied to the scabbard so that the swords can't be drawn."

"Huh."

I leaned down with interest at the hand guard...or rather, pretended to and used the opportunity to swing back and kick a spot on the water buffalo's side as hard as I could.

"Agha!" The water buffalo let out a bizarre yelp from the excruciating pain and let me drop. I took the chance to run off and disappeared into the crowd.

"G-get back here, you! Where did you go?"

Idiot. Like I'd get caught again.

Amid the cheers echoing for Iozen, Kumatetsu made light footwork around his opponent with his guard up in a low, boxing-style pose. With his sword slung over his shaggy upper body, he circled and constantly switched his guard up tauntingly. One moment he set off running on the spot in an almost dance-like performance, then suddenly twisted his body to show off a capoeira-like cartwheel going into a flip the next. The beasts in the square buzzed with approval, enthralled by his unexpected combination of skills. Kumatetsu added an extra capoeira cartwheel to thrill the crowd, then rotated his arm vigorously to answer their cheers.

"Kumatetsu's got some moves!"

"Awesome!"

"Give us more!"

Kumatetsu stuck his chest out proudly in response.

But Iozen remained calm and motionless during all of these provocations.

Seemingly amused by the comedy in this contrast, Tatara slapped his hands together with glee. "Ba-ha-ha-ha-ha!"

Beside him, Hyakushubo muttered, "What is that idiot doing?" with his head in his hands. He was apparently the type who felt easily embarrassed on behalf of others.

I watched from in between the beasts as Kumatetsu moved forward and backward, gauging his distance with nimble footwork.

Then—

Kumatetsu's left fist flew out abruptly at Iozen in a cross punch.

But Iozen evaded this with a simple backstep and sway.

As Iozen retreated, Kumatetsu pursued with his right and left fists, then switched his guard to deal out a combo of two left jabs, followed by a cross punch and roundhouse kick from his right. Iozen ducked to avoid these blows, and Kumatetsu stepped rapidly to immediately follow up with a fencing-like right jab, then a sharp strike with his left.

Still, Iozen expertly maneuvered his stance to avoid these attacks and put significant space between himself and Kumatetsu.

The crowd erupted in impressed applause at the sight of him anticipating and evading everything.

"Wow!"

"Now that's Iozen for you."

"He didn't even get hit once."

Casting Iozen a dauntless side-gaze, Kumatetsu gestured for him to come at him. The gesture said, "I'll do exactly what you just did, so bring it on." A murmur spread throughout the square—they doubted whether he could do such a thing. Iozen blinked as if to show a moment's hesitation, then lifted his fists. The blink seemed to say, "Are you sure you want me to strike?" Kumatetsu smirked in response.

Iozen started off the combo with his left fist, just as Kumatetsu had done.

With his guard down, Kumatetsu dodged the strikes with minimal backstepping, as if simply walking backward.

The crowd's audible astonishment seemed to please Kumatetsu.

In that split moment of distraction, Iozen's fist flew forward in a sharp strike.

It made a dull thud as it slammed into Kumatetsu's face.

"Oh!"

My face twisted in a pained expression.

Holding his banged nose, Kumatetsu no longer had the composure from before. His desperate eyes moved frantically as he avoided Iozen's attacks. His movements were exaggerated to a pitiful degree, so much that they enticed the audience's laughter as if they were for comedic effect. That didn't last long before Iozen landed another clean hit on Kumatetsu's unguarded, bloody-nosed face.

"Yes!" Ichirohiko and Jiromaru pumped their fists in the air.

"Idiot!" Hyakushubo muttered, appalled, while Tatara broke out in heedless laughter beside him.

"Ah-hee-hee-hee!"

Kumatetsu viciously shook his heavily bruised face to regain his senses. He sniffed the blood back up his nose and confronted Iozen, swinging wildly with all his might.

Iozen was waiting to counterattack, however, and a supple left kick exploded onto Kumatetsu's chest.

With a heavy crash, Kumatetsu's body slammed readily into the ground.

"No!" I yelled involuntarily.

Surrounded by the beasts' cheers and applause, Iozen lowered his guard, bowed briefly to his fallen opponent, and walked breezily away.

However, hearing the cheers turn into a buzz of commotion made Iozen turn slowly back.

It was Kumatetsu.

Despite having received such a critical kick, he was on his feet again, albeit staggering.

"...I'm not done yet!"

Heedless of the significant damage he'd taken, he still seemed more than ready to go. He moved the sword on his shoulder to his waist and hunkered down like a sumo wrestler preparing to charge.

The red fur on his arms stood on end with an audible blast. The fur on the rest of his body also bristled in succession, puffing his figure up to many times its original size.

"......!"

I gulped.

Kumatetsu had literally transformed into the form of a violent wild bear.

Ichirohiko anxiously let out a shout.

"Father!"

"No need to fear."

Iozen took his shirt off and placed his fingers on the ground.

His golden fur stood on end. Not only that, his fingers morphed into hooves. Letting the muscles and fur all over his body bulge, Iozen's appearance was now that of a wild boar.

I was dumbstruck by the beasts' shocking transformations.

But the audience must have been accustomed to this display, for they seemed to be enjoying the show. Referee-like, they all chanted, "Ready, set...," in unison.

"Fight!"

The two charged forward on all fours and crashed into each other head-on.

The ground reverberated from the impact with a boom. Wineglasses lined up on a stall clinked forcefully into one another.

Without pause, their enormous bodies slammed into each other at incredible speed.

Another tremendous crash shook the square. The dried stingrays hung for sale in a stall bounced up and down.

On their third collision, the two reeled backward from the force but regained their footing on the spot and locked arms with each other for the first time.

The sight of neither relenting in a competitive deadlock was like watching sumo wrestling.

Iozen was the first to gain the upper hand. He attempted to push through with sheer force, but Kumatetsu just barely managed to hold his ground on one leg. Kumatetsu teetered but somehow regained his balance, and then it was his turn to push with all his might.

"R...raaaaaar!"

Driven back, Iozen's sweat-drenched face twisted.

Kumatetsu grinned as if confirming his chance to win, then shoved as hard as he could with a cry of determination.

"Grrrrrrrar!"

Iozen's hind hoof slid on the cobblestones as it struggled to hold out. Though it appeared as if Kumatetsu's swollen thighs were revolving in vain, he was definitely pushing his opponent back. Iozen somehow held his ground at the very edge of the square just before the stalls. But his face was twisted in agony.

The audience let out a breath that sounded like a shriek.

"Iozen's in a fix."

"Is this it?"

Though Kumatetsu's face was covered in beads of sweat, he refused to give Iozen any slack.

As if reaching his limit, Iozen closed his eyes painfully.

But then—

"Come on, Iozen!"

A little beast girl riding on her father's shoulders raised her voice.

"?!"

This prompted more cries from the onlooking beasts.

"Iozen… Iozen…!"

The beasts' looks of concern dissipated as the cries grew in number, eventually becoming a giant chorus with fists pumping.

"Iozen! Iozen! Iozen!"

Everywhere I looked, they were cheering for Iozen.

"No one… No one's cheering for him…"

It gave me an idea of how the rest of the city regarded Kumatetsu.

"With all these beasts here, he's all alone…"

Iozen's eyes widened as if he'd been brought back to life by the mass of cheering, and he used all the energy he had left to push back and move forward. Slowly, yet surely. With each step, the crowd's cheers grew louder.

"U…urrg?!"

With an expression of disbelief at the unexpected turn of events,

Kumatetsu was pushed gradually yet undeniably back. Iozen drove forward harder and harder, and when he returned to the center of the square, he threw Kumatetsu off with a determined cry.

"Agck!"

Tossed away, Kumatetsu's body slammed onto the cobblestones and shrunk back to its normal size amid the rising dust.

Huge cheers erupted from all over the square.

"Yay!"

"That's Iozen for you!"

Iozen also returned to his usual form and stood up, his shoulders heaving as he caught his breath.

Meanwhile, still unable to get up off the ground, Kumatetsu panted as he reached for the sword knot at his waist with faltering hands to pull his weapon toward him.

"Still not done?" Iozen asked.

"...Not until I beat ya!"

Kumatetsu roughly undid the sword knot while holding on to the scabbard and slammed the blade vertically into the ground.

"Better for you to stop now."

Iozen's breathing was back to normal now, his voice calm and steady.

Kumatetsu used the sword for support to just barely pull himself up.

"Nah... This ain't over yet!"

Still gripping his blade, Kumatetsu leaned his upper body down slowly. Just when it seemed as though he would collapse, he shot out running and accelerated from that low stance, swinging the sheathed steel upward with all his might.

In a split second, Iozen undid his sword knot and pulled his sheathed blade out, blocking the attack.

The scabbards met with a reverberating hum. Kumatetsu's outrageous strength resulted in such an impact that even Iozen had difficulty keeping a grip on his hilt. Kumatetsu brought his sword down full-force for a second attack. Iozen met the blow mid-retreat, this time with both hands.

The vibrations echoed once more, and Iozen's entire body was swept back.

Panting heavily, the exhausted Kumatetsu looked as though he was just barely standing on his feet. Still, he readied his weapon.

Iozen also readied his sword in response.

The square echoed with the chanting for Iozen. But the two remained still, as if the air between them was dominated by silence. The lengthy standoff continued.

Kumatetsu was the one to break that silence.

The next moment, the two scabbards exchanged violent blows.

Throughout the all-consuming call for Iozen, I kept my eyes on Kumatetsu as he frantically swung his sword.

"……"

The power balance didn't last for long, and Kumatetsu quickly lost his edge. The sword slammed wretchedly into his cheek. Sweat splattered onto the cobblestones like rain.

"Get him, Pops!" Jiromaru shouted gleefully.

I just kept my eyes on Kumatetsu.

"……!"

Kumatetsu got slammed again and staggered pitifully. Although they were just blows from the scabbard, bruises were rapidly accumulating on his body.

"Ooh…!" Tatara covered his eyes involuntarily.

Hyakushubo's voice was a whisper, his face pale. "Kumatetsu…!"

I gritted my teeth and kept my eyes on him.

"……!"

Kumatetsu received a sharp jolt to his chin from below.

Sensing Iozen's imminent victory, the beasts raised their cheers to a climax.

As I watched them, I felt my body tremble with indescribable anger. I couldn't bear it anymore. I couldn't just stand by and watch in silence any longer.

I raised my voice as loud as I could.

"Don't give up!"

"?!"

Kumatetsu twitched.

Even over all the commotion, my words had clearly reached his ears.

The beasts murmured in confusion.

"Who's voice was that just now?"

"Who would have thought anyone would cheer for Kumatetsu?"

Covered in bruises, Kumatetsu looked searchingly all over the crowd.

And finally, he spotted me.

As if in reply, I yelled all alone from among the beasts.

"Don't give up!!"

Kumatetsu widened his eyes in surprise.

"...Kyu..."

Before he finished calling my name, the hilt of Iozen's sword rammed into Kumatetsu's face.

Crack! A deafening sound rang out, and Kumatetsu was blown into midair.

"Ooh!"

Tatara and Hyakushubo let out a yelp.

"That got him!"

Ichirohiko rejoiced in his father's victory.

Kumatetsu's body soared slowly, falling toward the ground.

Then—

"Enough!"

A voice rang out over the entire square.

Kumatetsu bounced on the cobblestones.

Suddenly, a figure with two long ears was standing between the two contenders, with arms raised to either side.

Iozen noticed immediately, quickly switched his sword over to his right hand, and bowed.

"Grandmaster."

All of the beasts in the square rushed to bow.

The beast they called Grandmaster was a rabbit. Strikingly short compared to Kumatetsu and Iozen, he was an elderly man with white fur and whiskers. Yet adorned in an extravagantly embroidered padded robe boasting a fluffy collar, he stood out more than any beast present.

"What is it you two are doing? It is too soon for the match."

The grandmaster spoke with authority, then hopped adorably like a bunny.

"I have not yet decided what kind of god I hope to become."

Iozen offered comment.

"Grandmaster. Please punish Kumatetsu for bringing a human into our midst."

"Hmm. But how much more is there to punish when you have already knocked him out?"

The grandmaster looked down with kindly eyes at Kumatetsu, lying facedown on the ground. Battered thoroughly and unable to move his body at all, Kumatetsu groaned as if to himself, "...Whatever anyone says, that kid's my apprentice..."

"I see. It seems he has the resolve."

Hearing the grandmaster's playfully oblivious tone, Iozen's eyes went wide with shock.

"You mean to allow an exception?! I'm sorry, but Kumatetsu cannot take on such responsibility!"

"The responsibility shall be mine. I am the one who pressed him to take on an apprentice, after all."

The grandmaster was suddenly behind Iozen. It was a mysterious maneuver, as if he had jumped through space. The bewildered Iozen looked over his shoulder and protested.

"But if he were to harbor the darkness..."

"It is not as if all humans are taken in by the darkness."

Faster than the eye could blink, the grandmaster now stood beside Kumatetsu. Iozen was having difficulty trying to protest.

"But...! Why are you always so easy on Kumatetsu?"

Even before he was finished, the grandmaster was outside the ring of beasts.

"That will be all. Disperse."

Iozen sighed heavily.

"Kumatetsu, be grateful for the grandmaster's benevolence," were the words he left behind before departing in long strides.

The beasts in the square dispersed randomly, returning to their respective jobs. I suddenly realized the sun had started its descent, and the light had shifted to the lazy rays of the afternoon.

I alone stood there, my eyes still on Kumatetsu.

When he finally managed to get up and noticed me there, Kumatetsu gaped at me for a while.

The next moment, however, he awkwardly averted his eyes.

The evening light enveloped Jutengai.

Covered in wounds, Kumatetsu miserably climbed the stairs back home. He stopped occasionally to howl at nothing in particular, seemingly frustrated that he had lost.

"Damn! *Rraaaaar!*"

I followed from a little distance behind, watching his back all the way.

By the time we got to the hut, the sun had set completely.

When I opened the door, the room was as chaotic as it had been that morning, and Kumatetsu was lying sullenly on the sofa with his huge back toward me. The sun emblem there seemed to have shrunk along with the sunset.

I spoke.

"You're strong."

Kumatetsu turned his face, covered in raw wounds, toward me slightly and said, "What fight were you watching?" before turning away once more.

I continued.

"If you promise I'll get strong by being with you, I'll be your apprentice if you want."

"...Hmph. You're just gonna run away again."

I chose not to answer, instead turning a chair on the floor upright to sit on, and looked at the eggs in the basket.

"These still haven't expired, right?"

Of course the eggs freshly laid that morning had to be okay to eat in the evening. I cracked one onto some of the cold leftover rice from the morning and grabbed some chopsticks to mix the stuff into a sticky mess.

Kumatetsu raised his head at the sound and peered at me from over his shoulder.

I hesitated a little bit. But then I steeled myself, closed my eyes, and threw some into my mouth with determination.

I chewed two or three times.

That raw smell I hated so much filled my mouth, and cold sweat erupted all over my body. *Oh no.* But with a surge of willpower, I forced myself to swallow.

Nausea immediately swelled up from deep within my chest.

"Ugh!"

Still, I summoned everything I had inside of me and turned my face toward Kumatetsu.

"T-tastes great…!"

Whatever. Raw smelling or not, I'd eat all of it. Bowl and all.

I noticed that Kumatetsu had turned toward me and watched with astonishment as I ate.

I had no idea what he found funny, but he was grinning with his eyes opened wide.

"Heh-heh. Right, Kyuta! I'm gonna train you good, so you better be prepared!"

It seemed his sulking from before had blown away somewhere. Kumatetsu arched back and let out a boisterous laugh.

I had other things to deal with, like fighting off the waves of nausea as I continued to eat through teary eyes.

"Urp… Ugh!"

Kumatetsu's laughter echoed beyond the hut.

That's how, from that day onward, I became "Kyuta."

THE
APPRENTICE

Hyakushubo taught me the usual way that all the men in Jutengai dressed.

Wear pants cropped halfway up the shins. Tie a sash around the waist. Tuck the shirt under the sash. Tying the sash on the left instead of the right was the Kumatetsu way, he added. He had even procured a set of used clothes for me from the market that fitted my short stature.

In a corner of the cluttered changing room, I took off the faded T-shirt I had been wearing and put my arms through the sleeves of a shirt made from unbleached cloth, put on some light green pants, and tied a crimson sash around me.

I was going to live among the beasts from now on, I told myself firmly.

Kumatetsu was waiting in the backyard.

Although it was called a "backyard," it wasn't actually a yard. The heavy stone building there apparently used to be an old warehouse, but now it was in complete ruins with the roof caved in, letting in the sunlight. A single young Bodhi tree twisted up from between the floor tiles to create a small area of shade. Kumatetsu used this space as he liked for training.

Next to Tatara, who was sprawled out on a bench with his head propped up on one elbow, Hyakushubo brewed some loose leaf tea with a portable tea set. A bird twittered somewhere, and a butterfly fluttered gently in the wind. It was a tranquil scene, as if we were on a picnic.

When I came out into the backyard having finished changing, Hyakushubo complimented me, saying, "Mmhm. Looks good on you, Kyuta."

"Shaddup."

Kumatetsu stopped him cold. He was staring at me uncomfortably in my training clothes. A human like me wearing beast clothing must have looked terribly wrong to him. But I felt just as awkward with myself in the outfit.

"Hmph."

Kumatetsu blew air out of his nose dismissively, then readied a simple stick in his left hand—just a branch broken off a tree.

"Watch what I'm about to do."

Apparently, he was going to show me some moves with the sword. I turned my attention toward him nervously.

Kumatetsu readied the stick high, then swung it down in one fell swoop.

"......?!"

I reeled back from the unexpected blast of air. Dried leaves and twigs rustled noisily up all at once. Every time Kumatetsu swept the stick up or sideways, the dried leaves in the air twirled in a different direction a moment later. Its power was so incredible; it was as if a tornado had been produced in that split second. Yet the trajectory drawn by the tip of the stick was infinitely smooth and gracefully efficient. It was like watching a dance performance with a real sword. How did he manage such a thing with just a normal stick?

"......"

I was stunned beyond words.

"Impressive. Very impressive." Tatara clapped lazily. "There aren't any geniuses on his level—aside from Iozen."

Even I, just a kid and a novice, had to agree with that. How much did one have to train to be able to control a stick at will like that?

Kumatetsu tossed the branch at me.

"Got that? Now you do it."

"Huh? What do you mean 'do it'?"

What you just did? Hold on. There's no way I can do that. That's impossible.

I was about to say so out loud when Hyakushubo urged me on with a smile while brewing his tea.

"Go for it, Kyuta."

It gave me a start. I had committed myself to living here now. I had to do it even if it was impossible.

Making up my mind, I swung the stick, trying to remember what I had seen.

"Hah! Yah! Yah!"

The branch that Kumatetsu had been flinging around like a twig moments before was heavy as iron in my hands. Still, I swung the best I could. I knew it looked nothing like what Kumatetsu had done. But I didn't care. As I swung the stick around with all my might, it suddenly slipped out of my hands.

"Whoa!"

The sound of it clattering on the tiles echoed pathetically. I heard a loud "pfft" as Tatara burst out in laughter.

Kumatetsu just kept looking at me in silence.

I was so embarrassed that I felt as though fire was erupting from my face.

But not letting that discourage me, I picked up the stick and continued swinging.

"Hah! Yah! Yah!"

I tried my best to make bigger swings this time. Then the tip swung around and smacked me on the thigh.

"Ow-ow-ow!" I grabbed my leg and hopped up and down.

Kumatetsu just kept looking at me in silence.

Uncomfortable sweat burst out and made my face all sticky.

Still, I swung the stick undeterred, or rather, obstinately determined not to quit.

"Yah! Yah!"

"…Cut it out."

"Yah! Yah!"

"Cut it out!" Kumatetsu bellowed to make me stop.

I was so embarrassed that it was all I could do to look up at Kumatetsu. Still, I summoned all of my spirit to speak up.

"Wh-what do I need to fix?"

Then Tatara, teacup in hand, threw a sarcastic comment my way in a voice loud enough for me to hear.

"Ha. 'Fix,' he says. That's a hoot."

"Wh-whadd'ya expect? It's only my first try."

"Bwa-ha-ha! First try! The widdle baby's first try! Bwa-ha-ha!"

Tatara's scornful laughter echoed relentlessly through the backyard as he joked around. I was at a loss for words. Tatara's words spoke for Kumatetsu himself. I deserved his scorn. Hyakushubo felt sorry for me and offered some support.

"You can't expect him to do it just by telling him to. Kumatetsu, explain to him from the beginning."

"Huh? Explain?"

"That's the duty of a proper master."

Kumatetsu seemed to mull over this for a while.

"…Fine."

With a sigh, he started off on his idea of an "explanation."

"So first you squeeze the sword like *hngh*, right?"

"Okay."

"Then you go, *whip*!"

"Whip."

"And *bang*!"

"……"

I was dumbfounded. All he had done was list some sounds.

However…

"See? You get it now, right?" was what Kumatetsu said in a satisfied tone. It was as if he was saying, *Easy, isn't it?* He seemed to think that he had explained things adequately enough.

"Huh...? Th...that's it?" I asked, and Kumatetsu's expression immediately clouded over.

"No, look."

"Okay."

"Hold it like *hngh*!"

"Like hngh."

"Go, *whip*!"

"Whip."

"And *boom*!"

"......"

"Right?"

Kumatetsu looked at me. His eyes said, *You have to have gotten it this time.* I was at a total loss. But at a loss or not, I had to try something.

"So like...hngh?"

"No, look."

I could hear the annoyance building in Kumatetsu's voice.

"*Hngh!*"

"Hngh?"

"No, no. *Hnngh!*"

"H-nngh??"

"No, no, no. *Hnnegh!*"

"H... Hnnegh??"

"No, no, no, no. *HNNERGH!*"

"Hnnergh!"

"*DHNNNNERGH!*"

"Dhnnnergh!"

"No! No, no! That's not it at all! Geez, you're a dense one!"

You're a dense one.

Kumatetsu must have said those words casually.

But I didn't take them that way. Those words blew away the last bit of self-esteem I had remaining in me.

The blood instantly rushed to my head.

"...I don't have to take this!"

"What?"

"You can't expect me to do anything by teaching like that!"

"Quit your griping and do it!"

"No!" I turned my back on him.

"Do it!"

"No!"

"Aw, son of a—!"

Kumatetsu ran his fingers all over his head in frustration.

Hyakushubo tried to smooth things over. "Kyuta's a beginner. Break it down a bit more…"

"Oh, fine then! I'll break it down for you nice and good!"

Kumatetsu grabbed his chest with his hand and closed in on me. "You grip the sword in your heart! You have one, right? A sword in your heart?!"

"Huh? Why would I?"

"The sword in your heart is what's important! Here! Right here!!"

Kumatetsu beat his chest over and over again with his eyes wide open, anxiously trying to get me to understand.

"Got that? Then do it!"

"……"

"DO IT!!"

"……"

Kumatetsu seemed to be waiting for my response. But I obstinately refused to turn around or answer.

Eventually Kumatetsu clicked his tongue, turned on his heel, and went out of the backyard.

"Where are you going, Kumatetsu?"

Hyakushubo stood up in a hurry and went after Kumatetsu, who was departing in long strides. "The fool, all he does is shout. Kumatetsu, wait. Kumatetsu…"

Kumatetsu and Hyakushubo disappeared from view.

"A sword in my heart? What the heck is that, moron?"

I swung the stick around in irritation. *What's with him? All he did was blabber nonsense. Is that all he can do—yell without explaining anything properly? I hardly got to do anything and he calls me "dense." The heck with that. Why would he assume that? He doesn't know me. Damn it. Stupid bear. Damn it. Damn it!*

"Hey kid... You should go back where you came from," said Tatara, the only one left behind.

"Huh?"

Tatara was no longer laughing or joking around. His tone was grave and severe. "An apprentice's training can easily last five, ten years. No way you're gonna last under Kumatetsu with such a flimsy attitude. If you just want a hand to feed you, get someone to care for you in the human world."

I could find nothing to say back to him.

"......"

"There's no place for you here. Better get the hell out on your own."

Tatara stood up and walked out of the backyard.

Only I was left behind, all alone.

After breakfast, Kumatetsu's hut was empty.

The chickens peacefully pecked at their feed in the front yard. Hyakushubo, who had come over randomly, was flipping the pages to his book of Buddhist chants while cooling himself off with a handheld fan.

But Kumatetsu was nowhere to be seen.

"...Where'd he go?"

"Who knows? He said something about being away for a day or two..."

Hyakushubo lifted his head and looked around.

I decided to come out and ask him.

"Tell me. What is an apprentice supposed to do?"

"What's this all of a sudden? Is this because of yesterday?"

"...Not really."

Still, it was true that what Tatara had said was weighing heavily on me. I knew now that coming up with excuses because I was a beginner or a kid was totally not going to cut it.

"Well now, you can start by cleaning, doing laundry, cooking—that kind of thing."

Hyakushubo gave me a brief explanation of what he thought an apprentice ought to do, along with some concise methods and tips required for each task.

Following his instructions, I pulled Kumatetsu's clothes off of the wire they hung on, one after the other, and took them outside, then carried all of the furniture and rugs and empty bottles and shoes in the hut out into the front yard.

The hut had no vacuum cleaner of any kind. I started sweeping, broom in hand. There was a ridiculous amount of dust, so much that I wouldn't have been able to stay there had it not been for the towel wrapped around my face. Hyakushubo hacked violently. Even the chickens rushed to escape the sheer amount of dust. How many years had this place not been cleaned properly?

Spots of grime that couldn't be removed with sweeping were caked all over the floors and walls. Most of it was alcohol and honey spilt from the empty containers that had dried out and hardened. After splashing water all over the hut to drench it, I got on all fours and scoured each of the spots away with a scrubbing brush, one by one.

The next day I started on the laundry. I separated the towering mass of clothes according to material. Obviously, the hut had no washing machine. The clothes had to be soaked in a tub and scrubbed on a washboard. It was the first time I had ever seen a board used for laundry. The pads of my fingers quickly became soft and wrinkled.

Hyakushubo taught me exactly how to go about each task in simple, concise words—how to sweep with a broom, how to wring a rag dry, how to scour with a scrubbing brush, and how to use the washboard. But probably for my own good, he never actually lent a hand in any of the apprentice's tasks. He would simply lean on the doorframe or have his cheek propped up on one elbow at the window, watching over me.

It was clear and sunny all the way to the horizon, making it a fine, perfect day to do laundry. I hung the laundry out on the clothesline on the roof. Hyakushubo sat behind me on a chair, fanning himself.

"Forget about Kumatetsu for now. He's quick to get angry but forgets everything by the next day as if it never happened. It's not worth your while to worry about it."

"I told you, it's not like that."

"Those'll get wrinkled that way. Shake them out more."

"Oh."

I followed Hyakushubo's advice and went back to shake the clothes out thoroughly.

The next morning, I went out to get groceries.

Though still early in the morning, the people working at the stalls were busy with their preparations.

I spotted Iozen in a corner of the square. He was giving out some kind of directions to his many apprentices. According to Hyakushubo, Iozen was a prominent figure in Jutengai who also sat on the council. The martial arts institution he oversaw, The Jutengai Guard, was evidently responsible for part of the city's policing activities. Iozen's face looked strong and reliable from the side. Yet the way he dealt with his apprentices was gentle in manner. I figured anyone would be happy to be an apprentice under a master like him.

A farmers' market sprung up in the morning square, filled with heaps of vegetables and fruits under colorful parasols. Since the farmers came to sell their produce directly, they could be purchased at slightly lower prices than the usual stalls. I went around the market with a list and some money in hand, both provided by Hyakushubo.

The vendors all stared at me with eyes mixed with curiosity and discrimination.

"I've never sold anything to a human before."

"I see."

At another stall, two female vendors, both elderly, asked me a bunch of questions to satisfy their curiosity. I accepted my groceries, making a point not to say anything I didn't have to.

"So, human, how long are you here for?"

"Dunno."

I mean, my guess was as good as hers. As I left, both arms heavy with baskets full of groceries, the women whispered loud enough for me to hear.

"Not very friendly, is he?"

"Well, he's only human, I suppose."

The women were obviously uncomfortable. But I was just as uncomfortable as they were.

If that was all I'd had to deal with, it wouldn't have been so bad.

On the way home, I was surrounded by Iozen's son, Jiromaru, and his band of buddies. They tried to drag me off somewhere with smirks on their faces. Reluctantly, I went with them. Their destination was a place where adult eyes wouldn't be there to intervene—a schoolyard.

Suddenly, Jiromaru shoved me from behind.

"You human! You monster!"

Jiromaru pushed me from behind over and over. With both of my arms holding the shopping baskets, he toppled me like a frog. Vegetables fell out of the baskets and scattered onto the sandy schoolyard. I had scuffed my cheek and lip, and I tasted blood.

Surrounded by his buddies jeering rowdily, Jiromaru smugly crossed his arms in front of his chest. I assumed Jiromaru was the leader of the gang.

"I heard my pops talking about him. He said humans are bound to get out of control."

"Whoa, really?"

"Watch, I'll get rid of him now before it's too late."

Jiromaru flung his fist up.

"Stop that, Jiromaru."

It was Ichirohiko who intervened.

"Brother!"

"What makes you think a weak little boy like this is going to become a monster?"

"But seeing weaklings like him just gets me all annoyed."

Ichirohiko lent me a hand to stand up. "The next time my brother does anything horrible, let me know. I'll scold him for you," he said gently and picked up my scattered groceries for me.

"I swear I'll get you if you tell on me!" Jiromaru barked, watching from behind.

"That's enough, Jiromaru."

"Brother's real strong, you know. He can make things float without touching them, like a shaman." Then he turned toward his older brother pleadingly. "Show him, won't you, Brother?"

"No. Powers aren't for showing off. You know how Father always says they're for kindness.

"I may be a kid now, but I'll train diligently and someday, I'm going to become a fine swordsman with a long snout and big tusks, just like Father," Ichirohiko exclaimed with admiration, looking up at the sky.

Jiromaru looked at his brother with twinkling eyes.

"Me, too! I'm gonna be an awesome swordsman like my pops!"

Ichirohiko turned around and gestured for his brother and his buddies to come with him.

I finished picking up my scattered groceries and turned to look at Ichirohiko.

The face I saw talking to his brother was charming. Pale skin and a handsome nose line peeked out from under his hat, which stuck up in the shape of ears. His eyes were filled with confidence. He must have been one of the elite among the beast children.

I couldn't help but feel upset. But not because Jiromaru had pushed me over or because his buddies had jeered at me.

It was because Ichirohiko had called me a "weak little boy."

It was true. I was weak.

"...Damn it."

I wanted to get stronger. As much stronger as I possibly could.

*   *   *

That evening, Kumatetsu returned home and immediately made a huge fuss.

"What the heck? Who did this? Who cleaned up without asking me?!"

"Your apprentice, of course," Hyakushubo responded matter-of-factly. He pointed out that the hut had gotten unbelievably clean while Kumatetsu had been away for a few days, that it was all thanks to his apprentice, and how he should be proud of me for it. But Kumatetsu didn't seem pleased. He scattered the beaded curtain as he barged into the kitchen and yelled:

"Don't you dare do anything unless I say!" with a ferocious expression on his face.

I was ladling some stewed ingredients into a dish and turned my face down so that Kumatetsu would see as little of my face as possible. But that apparently drew his attention toward something else.

"Eh...? What's that scrape doing on your cheek?"

Tatara swung by after work to join us for dinner.

Basically, the three beasts were all bachelors without families, and although each of them had their own places to sleep, it had always been their custom to gather at Kumatetsu's hut—their "hang-out spot"—to eat together or have a drink of tea or alcohol in one another's company.

The dish that Hyakushubo had taught me looked simple enough, but was actually quite an involved recipe. It had dried shiitake mushrooms, chicken dumplings, and yam cakes. Grilled tofu, daikon radish, and taro root. Finally, there were carrots. All of these were simmered separately, infusing each ingredient with the broth from the ingredients simmered before it. According to Hyakushubo, that was what brought out the delicate flavors of each ingredient, to avoid them all tasting the same in the end.

Such was the care taken to stew the flavors into these ingredients, yet Kumatetsu tossed them one after the other into his mouth without savoring them at all.

"Jiromaru got you? Ha. Pathetic. You should be ashamed for not getting him back. It's appalling, it is. Really, now."

This ticked me off.

"…Sure, I'm pathetic. I'm weak. Just like you say."

"As long as you know."

"But as long as we're talking, what about you?"

"What?" Kumatetsu's chopsticks stopped with a piece of daikon held between them.

"He's an early riser. You sleep till noon. He's busy. You're not. And yet you still do nothing."

I was telling him off in my anger.

Kumatetsu's chopsticks holding the daikon were quivering.

"By 'he,' do you mean Iozen?" Hyakushubo asked.

"He's busy but thorough. You've got nothing to do, but you're sloppy and careless."

"…So what are you saying?"

"I understand really well now why you can't win against him."

With these words, the daikon between Kumatetsu's chopsticks split neatly in two.

"What did you say, you little twerp?!"

Kumatetsu's roar was my cue to shoot out of the hut as fast as I could. Kumatetsu pursued from behind, his eyes narrowed with a look that could kill.

"You wait right there! Say that again!"

I went in a circle and entered the hut again from the entrance facing the front yard. Kumatetsu followed and sprang into the hut. From behind the table, I hurled all of my discontent at him.

"I'll say it as many times as I have to! You're just the worst!"

"What's that?!"

"Calm down, both of you."

Hyakushubo attempted to intervene, but Kumatetsu was having none of it. Tatara retreated against the wall with rice bowl and chopsticks in hand. I burst out of the hut again and ran around it. Kumatetsu bounded after me and also ran around.

"Who do you think you are, talking to your master like that?!"

"If you're gonna be a master, act like one!"

"What's that?"

"You get pissed over the smallest things."

"Hey!"

"You write things off as impossible and give up too quickly."

"That's might gutsy of you, giving me advice like that. But all an apprentice should do is shut up and listen to what he's told!"

"No way! If I listened to you you'd infect me with your stupidity!"

"Shut your mouth!"

"Let him off the hook, Kyuta," Hyakushubo shouted in a tortured voice. "Kumatetsu's just an overly difficult man. Try to be understanding."

"Kumatetsu, let's go outside, man. Okay? Come on."

Tatara led the raging Kumatetsu down the hill, trying to placate him all the way.

"Kumatetsu's anger then was out of control. He was so upset, he was stamping his feet on the ground. 'I'm being as thorough as I can for his sake, if you ask me! So what's with that kid?!' he yelled.

"So I told him, 'You've had enough, right? Just toss him out already.' But still he raged on. You know that place with the graffiti on the wall, just down the stone steps from the hut? The place with the solitary streetlamp lighting the way. Kumatetsu paced back and forth there, grumbling on endlessly and making me listen.

"'Besides, I've got plenty to do. I earn money working part-time chopping wood and doing plasterwork and picking tea. Even more now to account for him.'

"'Just give it up. That's the thing to do.'

" 'So why should I have to take that crap, eh?! Don't you agree?'

" 'Fair enough.' I was saying this with Kumatetsu's best interests in mind. 'You realize now how easy your life was before, don't you? The bachelor life is the way to go. There's no hassle, no responsibilities, and no getting angry over some hard truth you didn't want to hear.'

" 'Urg…'

"Kumatetsu jerked to a stop. Surprisingly sensitive, that guy.

"I made a show of shrugging my shoulders. 'Whoops. Didn't mean to say that.'

" 'Damn! Rrarrr!'

"Kumatetsu raged and punched the air vigorously.

"Just then—

" 'Good on you for training so late at night, Kumatetsu.'

"The grandmaster was suddenly there, sitting daintily on the small bench under the streetlamp.

" 'G-Grandmaster.' Kumatetsu backed away in surprise.

" 'It's a good lesson to show your apprentice how diligently you train yourself.'

" 'Er… Y-yes… Exactly what I was thinking.'

" 'Good. Then as a reward, I shall grant you this.'

"So saying, he handed Kumatetsu several envelopes.

" 'What are these?'

" 'Some letters of referral.'

" 'Referral?'

" 'Take your apprentice and set off on a journey touring the various realms. With these, you should have no problems meeting with the grandmasters of each place.'

" 'B-but…'

" 'All are famous for their wisdom. The journey should help you both discover what true strength is.'

" 'But sir…'

" 'Well, happy travels, then.'

" 'Wha—…!'

"Leaving Kumatetsu looking flabbergasted, the grandmaster was gone before we knew it.

"As I climbed up the stone steps, I mumbled loud enough for Kumatetsu to hear.

"'Man, it was the perfect chance to kick the kid out. But you can't very well ignore the grandmaster's bidding now.'

"And that, you see, is how we ended up setting out on a journey."

"Just because the grandmaster himself told Kumatetsu to set off on a journey with his apprentice didn't mean we could leave him alone with Kyuta when they were at each other's throats like that. Tatara and I felt we had no choice but to accompany them. The two of them kept squabbling at each other all the while we traveled down the highway, much to my weary astonishment.

"Kumatetsu sprung freely like a monkey through the overgrown primeval forest.

"Kyuta, on the other hand, was out of breath and had a difficult time simply climbing a tree. But whenever he lagged behind…

"'Hurry up!'

"Kumatetsu would yell at him, and Kyuta had no choice but to desperately keep up.

"Even faced with hundreds of stone steps, Kumatetsu leaped up them with ease.

"If Kyuta got exhausted and stopped to rest for even a moment…

"'Hurry up!' was what Kumatetsu would say. I would tell Kyuta to not worry about it and climb at his own pace, but then he would get back up, stubbornly refusing to give in. It must have been arduous indeed, but I imagine Kyuta must have built up a lot of stamina through all that.

"Lacking any sort of traveling funds from the outset, we never stayed at any of the merchant inns and usually slept out in the open. But we never wanted for food. At a mountain stream with a waterfall gushing into it, Kumatetsu leaned his head silently downward in pursuit of the elusive fish. The next moment, he was slapping rainbow char onto shore one after another, and very soon we had more than enough of a catch to eat. We savored the roasted rainbow char seasoned with salt, along with a soup flavored with some miso we had brought along. Beneath a sky filled with stars, the summer feast with all of us around a campfire was exceptional. But even that tranquility meant nothing to Kumatetsu, who wolfed down the rainbow char headfirst. He then looked at Kyuta, who was taking his time to eat.

"'Hurry up! Hurry, hurry, hurry!'

"That badgering riled Kyuta up, and he started chomping his food down to outdo Kumatetsu. He didn't even bother to listen when Tatara exclaimed that they should at least take their time and eat their food in peace."

"The first place we visited was a bizarre city on a raised piece of land crammed with lines of buildings. Despite being on barren land, it was famous for its special cultivation of plants, and it even had a huge flower market. If Jutengai is a city of cloth, this was a city of flowers.

"As soon as we presented our letter of referral, we were directed to the cave of the respected hermit who served as the city's grandmaster. Perched on an enormous wisteria tree with multitudes of flowers hanging down was a baboon-like sage in a cloak.

"'I humbly ask of your wisdom: What is true strength?' Hyakushubo asked with reverence.

"The baboon sage was a distinguished master of illusions.

"'Strength? I may lack in brute strength, but look, I am capable of producing illusions.'

"So saying, he held out a rose on the palm of his hand.

"Along came a small butterfly the size of a fingertip and landed on the flower. Then suddenly, the two merged into each other. The wings of the butterfly had become rose petals.

"The baboon sage giggled like a mischievous child.

"'Do not underestimate. At times, illusions can be closer to truth than reality.'

"Kyuta stretched his hand out in wonder toward the extraordinary flower petal butterfly. The moment his finger came in contact with it, the tiny butterfly blew up in size and was instantly bigger than any of us.

"'Whoa!'

"Even though we knew it was an illusion, that really knocked us off our feet!

"'That, you see, is what strength is. Ah-hee-hee.' The baboon sage bared his teeth and laughed with glee.

"The bastard Kumatetsu, however, seemed uninterested from the start and had his face turned elsewhere the entire time."

"The next place we visited was a curious city in a giant hole in a jungle, where the houses clung to the wall of the hole in rows.

"Why such a giant hole exists was obvious, considering the city's main industry. The region was famous for its ceramics, and it was a source of quality clay ideal for firing. The sheer size of the opencast pit suggested the lengthy history of the city. Its grandmaster, a sage who looked liked an aged long-haired cat, was using telekinesis to lift huge, diversely painted ceramic ware into a spiral in the air. As wide as the world of beasts is, it is an extremely rare opportunity to meet a sage gifted with the ability of telekinesis. As we gazed up in amazement, the long-haired cat sage spoke.

"'Strength? What is the point of seeking such a thing? I dabble in a bit of telekinesis, but however much strength I may possess, there is something I cannot overcome. You see...'

"'What is it?' Kyuta asked.

"'You there, excuse me.'

"'Yes?'

"'Come, will you not massage my lower back for me? Telekinesis doesn't help with the pain I have there. Ooh, ouch.'

"Blinking his grime-encrusted eyes, the long-haired cat sage painfully rubbed his lower back.

"Meanwhile, Kumatetsu alone showed no interest in the telekinesis and had his face turned elsewhere the entire time."

"The next city was a mazelike forest twisted into a spiral, and no matter how far we walked, all we saw were the thousands and tens of thousands of stone Buddhist statues lined along the path.

"Well, wondering where the sage's hermitage was, we first headed for a tower that looked like a temple, but the disciples there said that the sage wasn't in. We asked them where we could find him, but they clammed up and said nothing more. Apparently, that was just the way things were in that city. So we had no choice but to walk up and down the same paths. We searched everywhere but never found what we were looking for and were at a loss next to some stone statues on the side of the path. Suddenly, we noticed a shabbily dressed monk sitting there, crammed between two of the moss-covered statues. It turned out that this was none other than the grandmaster himself.

"The sage with the serene face of an elephant sat in the lotus position and spoke with a quiet voice like stones rubbing against each other. 'Strength? I am not the one you should be asking that question. All I do is sit in this spot day after day like stone, through wind or rain.'

"'Why is that?' Hyakushubo asked.

"'So that I may forget time, forget the world, forget my very existence, and transcend all of reality. That, you see, is...'

"'Is... Huh?'

"Mid-sentence, Kyuta realized that the sage he thought he had just been talking to had turned into a moss-covered Buddhist statue.

"'He has turned to stone,' Hyakushubo remarked softly.

"Starting with no one in particular, we put our hands together in prayer for the resting sage.

"Kumatetsu was picking his nose, however, and didn't even care to look our way."

*   *   *

"After being rocked on a boat for a while, we came to a peculiar island jutting out of the sea, with a city encrusted on its stony surface like small shells living off the rock.

"The grandmaster of this city—a seal-faced sage with a straw hat atop his head—sat on a balcony on the highest point of the island, with a fishing line that extended down to the ocean's surface many hundreds of meters below.

"'Strength? I am all for practicality.'

"So saying, the voracious-looking sage magically controlled his fishing rod to deposit a colorful amberjack he had caught into his wide, gaping mouth.

"'He who secures his catch before anyone else and savors all of the flavors of the world is the true winner.'

"With jagged teeth, he tore the amberjack apart headfirst and munched with relish, preaching to us in a friendly manner.

"'Sink your teeth in whenever you get the chance. That, you see, is…'

"'Is…?'

"The sage's eyes suddenly flashed, and he swallowed loudly. Kyuta and I instinctively sensed danger and retreated. But Tatara was just a bit late to notice.

"The sage seized the moment to fling his fishing rod with ferocious speed.

"'There's my chance!'

"Tatara was helplessly caught on the line. He struggled in a panic but it was already too late. Slipping out of his jacket, he fell in a beautiful arc toward the sage's gaping mouth.

"'AAAAAGH!'

"Tatara was done for. There was no saving him…at least that's what we thought. But the sage ignored Tatara himself and simply tossed the jacket caught on the line into his mouth and munched it up. He then flashed us a smile as we stood there, shaken.

"'No need to worry. I do not eat my guests.'

"It seemed to me that he was saying that he spared us so that we might experience the cruelties of the real world firsthand.

"Behind us, I heard Kumatetsu let out a giant yawn."

"A massive, heavy sun was about to set on the horizon.

"We trudged wearily through the wastelands to begin our trip back home.

"'Each of them just offered their personal theories, and they all said something different,' Hyakushubo groaned and sighed.

"Kumatetsu turned mockingly toward him.

"'What did I tell ya? You'll just lose sight of yourself by listening to all that babble.'

"*You think* that's *bad? I almost lost my actual self by getting devoured*, I thought. Kyuta alone seemed excited, holding his notes from the journey in one hand.

"'Strength has a whole bunch of meanings, huh? All of the sages had interesting things to say.'

"As expected, Kumatetsu snapped back. 'That so? Then why don't you sit your dainty little ass at a desk and enjoy your studies?'

"'Yeah, I'd learn a lot more that way, I bet. At least they don't say things like "zoom" and "hnnergh."'

"'True meaning is something you just find on your own!'

"'You just don't know how to explain things!'

"'Only because you're too dense!'

"'Oh, hell. Here they went again.

"'You two never run out of energy to bicker, I see,' Hyakushubo said, looking weary.

"'You can say that again. Give us a break, all right? Can't you see how tired we are?'"

"That night, we ended up sleeping out on the wastelands.

"Kumatetsu and Kyuta continued griping at each other over

dinner, so we wound up having to pitch two tents apart from each other.

"Under a sky full of stars, I watched over the campfire as I waited for Kyuta to fall asleep.

"But Kyuta came shuffling out of the tent. He had offered the poncho he had been wearing on the trip to Tatara, whose jacket had been eaten up. Though it was summer, the wastelands at night were cold.

"'Having trouble sleeping?' I asked as I poured hot water into the teapot.

"Kyuta hugged his knees and stared silently at the campfire.

"'...Do you figure I don't have what it takes?'

"'Is what he said bothering you?'

"'He says I'm dense.'

"'I don't think so. You didn't know anything about cleaning or laundry at first, but you got the hang of them as soon as I taught you a bit. You're a good student, and diligent and quick to learn.'

"'But...'

"I handed him the cup of tea I had poured and took out another cup from my tea set for myself. 'It's Kumatetsu who has the problem. Have you seen his technique? It's a mess. Or in other words, unique. Why do you think that is?'

"'......?'

"'He had neither parents nor master.'

"'What?'

"'He developed his strength all on his own. Unfortunately so. That's his talent and his misfortune. On one hand, he doesn't have to listen to anyone, but on the other, he can't give good advice to anyone, either.'

"'...I didn't know.'

"I took a sip of the tea I poured for myself and continued.

"'But sometimes, he can be strangely convincing. You know what it is I speak of?'

"'You mean when he said I should find the true meaning of strength on my own?'

"'Yes. I thought he had a point there.'

"'......'

"Saying no more, Kyuta just kept staring intently at his teacup..."

"Around the same time, Kumatetsu and I were lying around in our tent, staring at the flame in the lantern hanging overhead.

"'I just don't know how to teach him,' Kumatetsu muttered quietly.

"'To think the great Kumatetsu is so hung up over a cheeky little brat like him,' I jested, and Kumatetsu hastily denied what I said.

"'I-it's not like that!'

"It was the kind of night that was good for talking about the old days.

"'Well, if we're talking cheeky, you were pretty bad yourself as a kid. You had quite the mouth on you, even though you couldn't fight for your life.'

"'I just had no master worth learning from back then,' Kumatetsu said bitterly.

"'Yeah, aside from the grandmaster, no one bothered to deal with you, huh? They were quick to toss you aside just 'cause they thought you were a hassle for not following directions.'

"'Man, just thinking about those jerks now makes me angry.'

"'I hear ya. Just like what you're doing now. ...Whoops.'

"'Urg...'

"I wrapped myself in the poncho that Kyuta had offered me and closed my eyes.

"'Personally, I think the sooner the kid leaves, the better, but...if you intend to continue being his master, you'd best think back on how you really wanted to be treated when you were a kid, and good. Well, good night, then...'

"But Kumatetsu didn't sleep and, apparently, just kept staring at the light of the lantern."

TRAINING

"Squeak, squeak."

Chiko was jumping up and down and looking at me as if wanting to play.

But I had other things on my mind.

"Find true meaning on my own, huh?"

Ever since I had returned from our journey, Kumatetsu's words kept echoing in my head.

I had some idea of what he was trying to say. The way to strength wasn't something that could be taught step-by-step, nor was it written in a textbook. It meant I couldn't rely on anyone but myself to keep my eyes open and find that something that clicked. It's true that no two people/beasts are the same, and strength means different things to different people/beasts. Basically, I had to find out for myself what strength meant to me. I knew that, but still…

"I just don't know…"

Everyone was out that day, and the hut was empty. All alone, I lay down on my back. I could see the raindrops dripping from the eaves beyond the window.

"Squeak, squeak, squeak!"

Chiko climbed onto my chest and bounced adorably as if to beg.

Chiko, my head is full other things right now. I'll play with you later, so I wish you'd just wait a little bit…

Like Chiko would understand if I said that.

I scrunched my body up, pretending to be Chiko.

"Squeak, squeak, squeak! ...That's me pretending to be you, Chiko."

"Squee?"

Chiko cocked his head all the way over to one side, his mouth hanging open.

Whoops? Not even close, huh? I guess not. Ah well.

That's when I heard it.

A voice.

—*Pretend. As if you really were.*—

"?!"

I snapped my head up. I thought the voice sounded like my mom's.

I sat up and looked around the hut. Of course, no one was there except for Chiko and me—only the raindrops dripping quietly outside the window.

"...Was that you just now?" I asked Chiko.

"Squeak!" Chiko replied with a blink.

What had that voice been just now? I suddenly remembered that back when I was in nursery school, my mother had watched me copy everything my dad did and had said, "Ren, you're pretending you really are Daddy, aren't you?"

"Pretend. As if I really was, huh?"

I decided to try out an idea.

Kumatetsu was there in the front yard with his sword over his shoulder. He was very casually dressed, with just a jacket and cloth for underwear.

I stared intently at Kumatetsu from inside the hut.

"Pretend I'm really him...," I told myself. My idea was to pretend I was really Kumatetsu and try copying every move that he made while training. Plus, I would do it in secret without letting Kumatetsu notice.

Kumatetsu readied his sword with his right hand. I also readied a broom in place of the sword in my right hand.

Kumatetsu swiped the blade quickly to the left. I also swiped my broom to the left.

When Kumatetsu swiped to the right, I swiped to the right. When he swiped left, I swiped left.

Kumatetsu continued to swing his weapon without noticing me at all. *Good.* This was going well. I was going to copy every single move while he trained without missing a thing.

Then...

"Mmm...," sighed Kumatetsu, suddenly lowering his sword, and he scratched his utterly exposed butt with one hand. I had to copy every single move while he trained. I hastily scratched my own butt. Then...

"Yaaaawn."

Kumatetsu let out a huge yawn, still scratching.

As soon as I saw, I forced my mouth open and yawned. I had to copy every single move. Whatever it was.

"Huh?"

Without warning, Kumatetsu abruptly turned my way. He really had an animal's instinct (he *was* an animal, after all).

Oh no. Did he notice? I hastily hid behind the wall of the hut and held my breath.

Kumatetsu scratched his head and stared at the inside of the hut as if he sensed some strange reason to feel uncomfortable, but...

"Hmm..."

He eventually let out a confused grumble and went off somewhere.

It seemed he hadn't noticed after all. I sighed.

What am I doing? You call this training?

I had to worry about not getting caught before I even got around to copying him. But with such a small hut and front yard, it was impossible not to get noticed. What could I do?

Kumatetsu trained alone, using the full space of the front yard.

He flung his sword around against an imaginary opponent and repeatedly doled out kicks. It was a routine unique to Kumatetsu's style that went beyond the sword to freely incorporate strikes using the hands and legs. Despite his oversized body, his movements were gracefully fluid and amazingly left no opening for attack. There was no way I'd be able to copy it without him noticing. But I also couldn't hope to make any headway by just watching.

"......?"

That's when I noticed. The sweaty footprints from Kumatetsu's barefooted training were dotted in sequence over the tiles in the front yard. As Kumatetsu repeated the same routine over and over again, he placed his feet faithfully on the same spots every time, without fail.

I numbered the rows and columns of tiles in my head and memorized those spots.

Once night had fallen and I made sure that Kumatetsu had gone to sleep, I crept out into the front yard and outlined the spots I had memorized with some chalk to recreate the footprints.

I tried tracing those footprints, but our sizes were too different, and the length of each stride was hopelessly far. A small step for Kumatetsu was something I had to jump to reach. Still, it was a good way to study Kumatetsu's steps without being noticed. I tried putting my feet on Kumatetsu's footprints again and again. I didn't expect to be able to copy his upper body movements. But if I could just copy his steps… With that single thought in mind, I traced his footprints over and over again.

From then onward, I continued practicing in secret every single night.

At first, I struggled just tracing his footprints. But as I kept practicing, I felt like my body was gradually getting a feel for the timing and the way Kumatetsu moved his feet. The sequence of steps that had felt stifling at first slowly began to feel less so.

It was noon, and Kumatetsu was training like he always did in the front yard.

"Mmm. Hah! Yah!"

In this combo, he slashed his sword back in a flash, then twisted his body to kick.

Inside the hut, I also tried to do the combo.

"Mmm. Hah! Yah!"

As I struck out with my leg, my shin slammed into the side table with a bang.

"Ow-ow-ow!"

I held my leg in pain and hopped around.

"Hm?"

Kumatetsu suddenly poked his head into the room.

I looked at Kumatetsu with a guilty jolt.

Kumatetsu came into the hut toward me, obviously suspicious, and peered into my face with both of his hands stuck in his pant pockets.

"What was that? What are you up to?"

With his huge face thrust at me and nowhere to escape, I bent backward over the side table behind me.

"Uh...!"

He was grilling me, and I was stuck. Really stuck. *What should my excuse be? Uh...*

I saw Chiko looking up at me out of the corner of my eye.

Pretend. As if you really were.

I thought I heard my mom's voice in my head.

Oh, the heck with it. There's no way I can keep copying him without getting noticed! Feeling reckless, I shoved my hands into my pant pockets the same way Kumatetsu was doing in front of me.

"Wha—?"

Kumatetsu muttered blankly, then involuntarily sniffled his nose with a snort.

I sniffled my nose with a snort just as Kumatetsu had done.

"Eh?"

Apparently onto something, Kumatetsu moved his shoulders around on purpose.

I also moved my shoulders around just as Kumatetsu had done.

Kumatetsu cracked his neck from side to side.

I also cracked my neck from side to side.

Kumatetsu thrust his left hand in the air in an attempt to throw me off.

I thrust my left hand in the air frantically to keep up.

Kumatetsu quickly thrust his right hand up.

I also thrust my right arm up.

"......"

"......"

Kumatetsu and I glared at each other as we gauged each other's next move.

"Eh?"

"Eah?"

"Huh?"

"Huhh?"

"Hup!"

"Whup!"

Unbeknownst to us, Tatara had come up to the window and was watching us, speechless. "What the heck are you guys doing?"

Coming to his senses with a jolt, Kumatetsu yelled at me.

"You making fun of me?!"

"Am not!"

"Then what are you doing?!"

"Nothing you need to know!"

Kumatetsu paced around the hut in irritation. I stuck right behind him like a suckerfish. When Kumatetsu swung around, I swung around. When he stopped, I stopped.

"Geez, that's annoying!"

No longer able to stand it, Kumatetsu burst out of the hut as if in need of escape. I rushed to follow him but lost sight of where he had gone.

I made a decision then. No more secret training. I was going to latch on now, no matter how annoyed he might get.

"Having made his escape, Kumatetsu pressed himself against the wall outside of the gate, ninja-like, and peeked back at Kyuta.

"'Geez, what the heck?' he muttered with a sigh. He didn't seem to understand what Kyuta was trying to do at all. Being the helpful man that I am, I gave him a simple analogy.

"'You two are like duck and duckling.'

"'I ain't no duck, Hyakushubo.'

"'It's only natural for a child to grow by imitating his parent.'

"'Ain't no parent neither.'

"'Kyuta means to learn from you. Like an infant following his parent.'

"'An infant...?'

"Kumatetsu continued to roll the word 'infant' in his mouth for a while. Perhaps it resonated with him in some way.

"The duck analogy was something I came up with on the spur of the moment, but now that I had mentioned it, I thought it was rather accurate. They say a duckling freshly hatched after breaking through its shell instinctively thinks that the first thing it sees is its parent and follows it around—even if that thing isn't actually its parent, merely a toy or some other piece of junk. The very first perception of the world that a child faces is the parent. It's through the parent that the child encounters and learns about the world. The existence of a parent is essential for a child's development, even if that existence is not genuine.

"Given Kumatetsu just happened to be the first thing that the lonesome Kyuta encountered in the beast world, perhaps such a thing was possible. The beast Kumatetsu and the human Kyuta—it wasn't impossible for a father-son relationship to be forged that transcended species.

"Of course, Kumatetsu had never been a parent, nor had he been blessed with parental love in his past. If anything, he was the exact opposite of what most would consider a parent. If it was possible for a man like him to become someone's parent, perhaps that was my chance to get a sense for just how profound this world can be. So thinking, I reveled in my own clever analogy, spontaneous as it had been.

"It was true that Kyuta and Kumatetsu's relationship, which had been nothing but hostile, changed slightly.

"Kumatetsu went out into the front yard for his usual morning training. Kyuta peered out at him as he swept with a long-handled broom. Feeling Kyuta's eyes on him, Kumatetsu raised his sword high and begin his training. Taking care not to be too conspicuous, Kyuta frantically followed the movement of just Kumatetsu's feet.

"I didn't miss the expression that Kumatetsu made just then. Glancing at Kyuta behind him, he let slip a satisfied little grin, as if to say:

"*Ha. So he suddenly came around, eh?*

"They say that any parent would be delighted to see their child imitating them, and I wondered how the two of them would change from here on out. I smiled to myself, feeling like I was privy to a surreptitious science experiment. But at this point, I was the only one letting my thoughts wander that way. Tatara still showered Kyuta with sarcasm as he had always done.

"'Hey, kid. How long are you gonna fool around like that? You think anyone would train if all it took to get strong was to be a copycat?'

"But it was none other than Kumatetsu who put a stern stop to that.

"'Hey, Tatara! Don't distract him!'

"Tatara blinked.

"'Wha—? But you wouldn't shut up about how annoyed you were having him follow you around…'

"'Just stay out of the way, will you?'

"Having been yelled at, Tatara escaped through the beaded curtain into the kitchen and found me leaning against the sink, sipping tea.

"'What? Since when'd he become a changed man?'

"'Who knows? I suppose he inevitably found affection for his eager apprentice.'

"'Yeah, right. As if that bastard's capable of that kind of thing,' he snickered, but then abruptly turned back toward Kumatetsu with a serious expression on his face.

"'...You're serious?'

"It seemed Tatara, too, realized what Kumatetsu's change in attitude meant.

"From that point on, Kyuta worked so hard it was almost heartbreaking. He imitated Kumatetsu's leg movements from morning to night. This obviously included training time out front and out back, but he also followed Kumatetsu around everywhere else, watching his feet intently. At some point, I noticed that the way Kyuta climbed the stairs was now exactly the same as Kumatetsu's bowlegged waddle. I thought that seemed a bit far, but Kyuta's 'secret training' was about to produce some sudden results.

"From here on is what Kyuta himself told me afterward.

"That day, Kyuta was starting preparations for dinner as he always did. From the kitchen, Kyuta could hear the voices of Kumatetsu betting on a card game against Tatara on the bench in the front yard. Fresh out of the bath after his part-time job, Kumatetsu often spent his time until dinner relaxing a little like that. Kyuta half listened to the two of them talking as he removed the eyes from the potatoes with the base edge of his knife. Kumatetsu seemed to have gotten a favorable hand.

"'Oh ho, there we go!'

"'Whoa, hold up.'

"'No way.'

"'Wait, wait.'

"'Nope. Heh-heh.'

"Kumatetsu stood up from the bench and retreated a few steps.

"Kyuta's feet naturally moved backward in time with that rhythm. By this time, Kyuta was so focused on Kumatetsu's feet all day that his own feet would move involuntarily even when he wasn't trying to imitate.

"'You've gotta be kidding me,' came Tatara's anxious voice.

"'Hee-hee,' Kumatetsu laughed playfully, dodging to the left with quick sidesteps like a crab.

"In that very same rhythm, Kyuta sidestepped to the left in the kitchen.

"Kumatetsu moved his feet to the right to dodge Tatara.

"*Steppity step.*

"As he removed the eyes from the potatoes, Kyuta also moved his feet to the right without so much as a thought.

"*Steppity step.*

"This was when Kyuta realized what was happening.

"'...Huh? But I'm not watching him...'

"Kumatetsu was in the front yard, and Kyuta was in a far spot inside the hut, in the kitchen facing the sink. The front yard wasn't visible from the kitchen. He could only hear sound.

"In other words, Kyuta hadn't seen anything.

"He hadn't seen, and yet he could tell how both of Kumatetsu's feet were moving.

"'...I can tell.'

"Kumatetsu made a pompous show of placing his right foot on the bench.

"Kyuta hadn't seen, but he somehow knew it was the right foot and not the left.

"'...I can tell!'

"A drop of water fell from the faucet into an enameled pot, creating a ripple. Kyuta himself was startled by the effects of his secret training, but his surprise soon turned to conviction.

"The sounds of Tatara bitterly slamming his cards down and Kumatetsu laughing smugly with one foot up on the bench echoed into the kitchen. Kyuta could image Kumatetsu vividly, as if he was physically there.

"He hadn't seen, yet he could see.

"'...Time to test it out,' Kyuta muttered to himself, quietly devising a plot in his mind."

"I had no idea that any of this was going on.

"That's why the morning it happened, I didn't even notice that there was something different about Kyuta as he snuck up stealthily on Kumatetsu, who was doing his stretches in the front yard.

"Kumatetsu was lazily stretching out his Achilles tendon when Kyuta, turning the handle of his broom, suddenly jabbed him in the side.

"'Ow!'

"Kumatetsu was caught off guard and stumbled a bit.

"Hyakushubo and I were stunned.

"Taking no heed, Kyuta just kept on jabbing Kumatetsu.

"'Whadd'ya think you're doing? Cut that out.'

"Of course, being jabbed by a kid didn't hurt Kumatetsu in the slightest. But Kyuta was so relentless with his jabbing that Kumatetsu couldn't stand the frustration anymore and made a move to grab the kid.

"'...Cut it out!'

"But then—

"Kyuta slipped easily past Kumatetsu's hand.

"'...Eh?'

"Kumatetsu attempted to catch Kyuta again, using both hands.

"But what do you know? Faster than he could, Kyuta had circled around behind him.

"'Eh? Wha—? Huh?'

"Even as Kumatetsu turned to catch him, Kyuta was instantly behind him again, as crazy as that sounds. Kyuta dodged Kumatetsu so amazingly well that I just stopped and stared with my jaw open, as if seeing magic with my very own eyes.

"'How the heck…?'

"'Kyuta, you…'

"Kyuta explained without stopping. 'I kept copying him by looking just at his feet. Then I realized I could kinda tell what was coming next. Once I could tell, I could dodge him.'

"Hyakushubo seemed flabbergasted but impressed nonetheless.

"'Incredible… Easily said, perhaps, but how much concentration does one require to pull off such a feat?'

"Kumatetsu struck out with his fist from an awkward position, irritated at not being able to catch Kyuta.

"'Stop messing with me!'

"His fist only met air and didn't even graze Kyuta. This made Kumatetsu lose his balance, and he slammed his chin smack into the ground.

"Honest to gods, I was amazed. I had only thought of Kyuta as a brat and nothing more, but after seeing him do something like *that*, well… A reevaluation was in order.

"I called out to him with newfound respect.

"'That's mighty incredible, Kyuta! For the first time, you've really got me impressed!'

"Now that I think about it, that was the first time I called Kyuta by his name. This threw Kyuta off for a second, but then he flashed a truly happy smile at me.

"I said to Kumatetsu, 'Kumatetsu, you'd better start learning from Kyuta.'

"'…Learn?! Why should I do that?!'

"Kumatetsu sprang up and yelled, letting his anger rage.

"Kyuta responded with intentional self-importance.

"'I can teach you if you want, but in return…'

"'What's that?!'

"'In return… I have no idea how to hold a sword or throw a punch, so…teach me, won't you?'

"Kyuta sounded surprisingly insecure, but that made his desperate look at Kumatetsu all the more compelling.

"Even now, I remember that look in Kyuta's eyes really well.

*   *   *

"From there, the training really started.

"Kumatetsu gave Kyuta lessons every morning, before even the cicadas were out screeching. Wielding a wooden sword with cloth wrapped around it, Kumatetsu would casually deflect Kyuta's sword and gauge his timing to strike Kyuta on the head.

"'Ow!'

"'Ha.'

"'Damn it. You need to teach me better!'

"But Kyuta wasn't only taking his licks.

"After breakfast, it was his turn to instruct Kumatetsu.

"Kumatetsu had his hands tied with cloth wound tightly around them, limiting his movements. Then Kyuta's wooden sword made a clean hit on the top of Kumatetsu's head.

"'Ow!'

"Kyuta slung the wooden sword over his shoulder.

"'Watch your opponent carefully and match your movements.'

"No sooner had he said that than he slammed another strike into Kumatetsu's leg.

"'Ow!'

"'Match your movements.'

"'Ow!'

"His yell went falsetto from the pain.

"Hyakushubo and I were enjoying a leisurely breakfast of toast and coffee as we observed Kumatetsu getting thrashed.

"'Watching him like this really exposes his weaknesses, doesn't it? You can tell just how heavily he relied on attacking up until now.'

"'Well, he's a self-centered prick who doesn't give a damn about anything around him, after all. Matching someone else has got to be harder than anything he's ever done.'

"'That's what he gets for getting stronger all on his own.'

"Kumatetsu continued to get beaten. Kyuta put his hands on his hips and voiced his criticism.

"'I said, match your movements to your opponent.'

"'I'm doing that!'

"'Then you're not doing it very well.' Kyuta remained unfazed.

"'Why, you pompous little…!'

"Kumatetsu's teeth grated noisily, and his face twitched with anger. But he stopped himself just before he snapped and, in a strained voice, said:

"'…You need to teach me better.'

"You should know that Kyuta's training wasn't just about sword fighting. Weaponless combat was an integral part of Kumatetsu's style. Facing a small watermelon stuck on a bamboo rod, Kyuta thrust his fist into it with a short yell.

"'Yah!'

"But the watermelon only bobbed back and forth without so much as a scratch. Without a steady strike, breaking open something like that isn't easy.

"Voicing his pain, Kyuta shook his swollen red hand and waited for the pain to pass. Well, that was about right for a beginner.

"But for an expert like Kumatetsu…

"'Hiyah!'

"One strike was all it took to pulverize an earthenware pot of water so big we could barely fit our arms around it.

"'Damn it!'

"This fueled Kyuta's competitive urge, and he was determined not to lose.

"Even in Jutengai, it was rare for a kid to receive proper martial arts training. By the time Kyuta started looking comfortable in his training wear, none of the kid beasts were a match for him anymore.

"In particular, the flimsy punches that his former bullies threw were like a joke to him. Without so much as touching his opponent, Kyuta simply sidestepped him, and the kid would miss and fall flat on his face of his own accord. This wasn't just against one opponent. Whether against a double-teamed punch or surrounded by a whole lot of them, Kyuta nimbly dodged them all and never once lost. His ranking among the children of Jutengai shot up like crazy. Then one day…

" 'Don't get too full of yourself, you!'

"Jiromaru blocked Kyuta's path with a skewer of sweet rice dumplings in one hand. He trained along with his older brother at Iozen's dojo and was so skilled that he was allowed to carry a sword despite still being a kid. None of the other kids doubted that Jiromaru would thrash Kyuta to a pulp. The usual gamble-loving trio also found themselves in another deadlock.

" 'I say Jiromaru.'

" 'I say Jiromaru, too.'

" 'Same here.'

"But seriously, who bets on a fight between kids, anyway?

" 'Take that, and that, and that!'

"Jiromaru sprang at Kyuta with a barrage of wild punches.

"But those punches didn't so much as graze Kyuta.

" 'Why, you little…!'

"Jiromaru swung the stick of dumplings out from between his teeth. Two dumplings slipped off of the stick and flew right at Kyuta.

"*Slap, slap!* Kyuta beat them back with the palm of his hand.

"Rising up to the challenge, Jiromaru sent them straight back with his own hand.

"The dumplings zoomed back and forth between the two at blinding speed. The closer the two got, the faster the rally became.

"Kyuta's strike with the heel of his right palm forced both of the dumplings into Jiromaru's mouth.

" 'Urg!' Jiromaru gasped.

"Kyuta followed up by dropping his center of gravity and pushing his opponent's chest with a strike from the heel of his left palm.

" 'Whoa!' Jiromaru landed with a bump on his ass.

"That was the match. Kyuta had won. He made a brief bow, observing the proper formalities.

"The gamble-loving trio cursed at the unexpected outcome, and the onlooking kids raised a cry of astonishment.

"Wide-eyed with amazement, Jiromaru chewed the dumplings in his mouth and swallowed with a gulp.

"'You're pretty awesome,' he said in an impressed tone, beaming at Kyuta. Now it was Kyuta's turn to widen his eyes at Jiromaru's sudden change.

"'Huh?'

"Standing up, Jiromaru held out both hands to shake Kyuta's.

"'See, I like strong guys. You come over to my house sometime. I have a lot of yummy snacks there. Promise you'll come by, okay?'

"His cheery, innocent smile totally took Kyuta off guard.

"Winter came and spring went by, and summer came 'round again. By that time, it was customary for us to eat watermelons cracked open by Kyuta's fist. As always, Kumatetsu and Kyuta competed with each other every chance they got. They even raced to see who was faster at eating watermelon.

"'Didn't I tell you two to take your time when you eat?'

"But they didn't lend an ear to anything I said. Having finished eating a moment faster, Kumatetsu stood up, throwing his rind to one side. 'I win! Good luck with the dishes.'

"Someone had decided at some point that the loser had to do the cleaning up. Of course, that meant Kyuta did it most of the time.

"One day, I overheard Hyakushubo talking to him in an impressed tone with one hand on Kyuta's head.

"'You've really grown quite a bit.'

"'You think so, Uncle Hyaku?'

"Realizing something, I ran up to them.

"The top of Kyuta's head was taller than mine, even standing on my toes.

"'When did that happen?! Are you serious?!'

"Seeing him every day made it hard for us to notice, but he had suddenly grown a whole bunch. Even though his face hadn't changed one bit, you know? You honestly can't underestimate how fast a kid can grow on you.

"'Uncle Tata.'

"Kyuta had come to call me that by that point.

"You know that single tree growing in the middle of the backyard? That Bodhi tree, I mean. Kumatetsu and Kyuta often trained under that tree. The tree was young and frail at first, but its leaves colored, snow fell on its branches, then it eventually flowered and started to leaf out from new buds. Just as the trunk of the Bodhi tree got thicker and thicker, Kyuta's frail little arms built up agile muscle. Time really goes by so fast. That Bodhi tree is huge now, and every time I see it, I'm reminded of Kyuta growing up.

"To tell you the truth, nobody—including me and Hyakushubo—thought that Kumatetsu would be any good at looking after an apprentice. But then rumors started springing up. Even though Kumatetsu seemed to be his same old self, the way that his human apprentice improved was pretty incredible, they said. As the days and months went by, those rumors produced more rumors. Before long, Kyuta was considered one of the city's best young swordsmen—the talk of everyone in Jutengai.

"Word of Kyuta's accomplishments reached the grandmaster's ears, too. He apparently went out of his way one day to see Kumatetsu and Kyuta's evening training, bringing Iozen with him.

"Iozen was amazed at Kyuta's development. 'Impressive. His moves are actually decent.'

"'It certainly seems that way,' the grandmaster said fondly.

"'He did well to train a human child so well.'

"'Oh? Not even you notice, then?'

"'Sir?'

"'Kumatetsu is the one who has grown. His moves have become sharper and more refined.'

"That remark made Iozen pay closer attention. '…It's true, now that you mention it!'

"'Who can say who the master is now, eh? Ho-ho-ho!' the grand-master said with a knowing laugh. They say his laugh then sounded so happy.

"But Kumatetsu himself had no way of knowing this. At the end of that training session, Kumatetsu asked Kyuta a question.

"'Kyuta. How old are you now?'

"Still in his fighting stance, Kyuta held up ten fingers, then seven.

"'Fine. Then from here on out, you're Junanata.'

"'Kyuta's fine with me,' Kyuta replied dismissively, then bowed, motioning for Kumatetsu to do the same.

"Kumatetsu reluctantly made a bow.

"As they talked, a vast sunset enveloped the two of them.

"Spring.

"Kumatetsu-an had wave after wave of young beasts coming in, wanting to be apprentices.

"'Master Kumatetsu! Please make me your apprentice!'

"A hopeless-looking, pimple-faced kid pleaded desperately, bowing down low with his knees on the ground. It was my job to deal with these kids.

"'All right. I like your determination. You've got potential, kid,' I'd say, or something random like that.

"'Thank you! I want to get to be like Mr. Kyuta!'

"'I hear you. Now, get in line over there,' I said, pointing with my chin at the lengthy line of would-be apprentices, stretching far down the stone steps. Pimple-face answered with a spirited 'Yes, sir!' and rushed all the way to the back of the line. I added a bit of important information at the end.

"'As you wait, make sure you're ready to pay your commission.'

"My thoughts wandered as I gazed at the long line. Not one of those fresh-faced kids looked like they would ever amount to much.

"Still, there was no denying that this was Kumatetsu-an's first-ever chance to rake in the cash. I did a head count of the kids lined up with their idiotic faces and did some multiplying. They were all here to learn from Kumatetsu because they wanted to be like Kyuta. If we took a monthly fee from them all, Kumatetsu wouldn't have to work part-time doing plasterwork or picking tea anymore. No, even better, he might even be able to move out of that dirty little hut of his and rent a new, bigger space. No, no. Forget renting. He might even be able to build a dojo of his very own. Then Kumatetsu would be a property owner. A man of substance. A fat cat.

"But Kumatetsu didn't care about any of that. He just continued to eat his lunch, arguing with Kyuta. Nothing about them had changed in eight years.

"'What did you say, Kyuta?'

"'I'll decide how I train on my own!'

"'No, do as I say!'

"'No way!'

"Hyakushubo interjected in an attempt to reason with Kumatetsu. 'Kyuta's an adult already. Treat him as such.'

"'Him? When he's all bare with no hair on him?!'

"'I do, too, have hair!'

"'Where?!'

"Honestly, these two would argue over the most useless things.

"Still, I have to say I understood how Kumatetsu felt then. No matter how big Kyuta got, in Kumatetsu's eyes he was still no different from when he was a kid. And he wanted to keep it that way. But kids, you just can't keep them from becoming adults.

"Kyuta finished eating a hair before Kumatetsu and left the hut, saying, 'I win. Good luck with the dishes.'

"'Hold it! I'm not done talking.'

"Kumatetsu rushed after him.

"Kyuta went down the stone steps at full speed, glancing at the line of hopeful apprentice prospects out of the corner of his eye.

"Jiromaru, who had come to take a look at the line, spotted Kyuta and called out to him.

"'Hey, Kyuta! Come stop by my place!'

"'Later!'

"Being pursued by Kumatetsu, Kyuta ran by without stopping.

"Jiromaru was a year younger than Kyuta, so he was sixteen or seventeen by then. Although his roly-poly figure and unibrow remained the same, his former rascally personality had faded along with the juvenile boar markings on his head, and his face looked calm and reliable now. Ever since the fight involving the dumplings in their youth, Jiromaru and Kyuta had been the best of friends.

"Jiromaru rubbed his impressive tusk that had grown out over the years and turned to Ichirohiko next to him.

"'Kyuta's really something. Kumatetsu-an's doing really well thanks to him. Old pops said even our Jutengai Guard's got to stay on its toes.'

"Ichirohiko was a year older than Kyuta at eighteen. He might have been even taller than Kyuta. His former well-mannered sweetness had been replaced by the gallant features of adulthood. But his eyes now had a kind of shadowy glint to them that hadn't been there when he was a kid. Plus for some reason, he always had the end of his scarf pressed against his mouth as if to hide it.

"'Kumatetsu? Hmph. Don't compare Father with that outcast,' he spit out bitterly.

"The bottom half of Ichirohiko's face from the nose down was always and unfailingly wrapped tightly with his scarf. There were various rumors going around as to why he dressed like that. They said he had a burn there or something. But nobody knew what the real reason was.

"Anyway.

"I just gave you a general idea of what happened up to when Kyuta turned seventeen, but are you guys keeping up with the story so far?

"After Kyuta ran out of the hut having had a spat with Kumatetsu, he would chance upon an extremely important encounter. An encounter so incredible, it would completely change Kyuta's future forever.

"It wouldn't be right for me to tell that story in my own voice.

"Let me go back to telling it in Kyuta's words."

KAEDE

With Kumatetsu coming after me, yelling his head off, I ran frantically through every alleyway and backstreet in Jutengai to get away.

Back when I was short, it had actually been much easier to escape him. There were plenty of ways to get around the alleyways that Kumatetsu's huge body couldn't fit through, like a low hole in a wall or a narrow gap in a doorway. But as I gradually grew, I found that I could no longer fit through them myself. So now it was a matter of speed. All I could do was get away as fast as I could.

I finally stopped hearing his bellowing beyond the alleyway, and I put my hands on my knees to rest for a moment.

"Man, he's persistent…"

As I looked behind me and caught my breath, out of the corner of my eye I glimpsed some flowers placed on a stool. It was an arrangement of camellias in a dish. Camellias, symbolizing the end of winter and the beginning of spring. The great camellia tree of legend has a spring lasting eight thousand years and a fall lasting eight thousand years…

Then—

A bustling sound I had never heard before reached my ears.

"Huh? What is this place…?"

No, I had heard it before. I remembered it from long ago.

The commotion grew louder.

I lifted my face and strained my eyes.

Beyond the alleyway, something was flickering in the hazy warmth of spring.

The commotion was now deafening.

"……!"

This wasn't Jutengai anymore.

Flickering in the haze was the sight of a bustling intersection filled with a startlingly huge moving crowd—of *humans*.

Shibuya after eight years seemed like an utterly alien world to me.

It failed to evoke even the slightest bit of nostalgia in me. The many buildings, the many windows, the many screens, the many rows of cars—all of them felt surreal and distant, not to mention empty. In particular, the sheer amount of writing that filled the city bore down on me with sickening unfamiliarity. Taglines, product names, explanations, messages on etiquette, warnings—everything was displayed in writing, cramming every last bit of space with excessive information. I couldn't help but question the need to rely on writing this much.

Another problem was that I couldn't read most of it. The onslaught of strange lettering that leaped into my field of view only fueled my anxiety, and I was even starting to feel a bit sick.

Of course, I learned basic reading and writing at the school in Jutengai. But the beasts' belief was outlined with the saying: "I cannot see why living knowledge should be recorded by a lifeless medium such as writing—pictures are more befitting the attempt." And but for a few exceptional students like Ichirohiko, literacy in the beast world was nothing compared to the human world.

I was a complete outsider. Despite the sheer number of people passing by me, I shivered with a penetrating sense of isolation. I didn't belong anywhere in this world. I gulped back my uneasiness and walked among the crowds with nothing to turn to.

I ended up in a corner of the residential area beyond the center of the city, in front of the small brick-colored ediface of a public library.

Gentle light came in through the skylights, adding contrast to the neatly lined books. Inside it was quiet, with only a handful of visitors. The substantial absence of people compared to the city center was an incredible relief for me. I still felt a little nauseous from all the writing I had seen. I was through with having writing forced into my face and figured it would at least be better to look at writing I was familiar with. Then perhaps I would remember what I knew as a kid. But that was easier said than done. I couldn't even find one book I remembered reading in the past. Discouraged, I decided to wander through the shelves.

I took a random thick book off the shelf and read aloud what phonetic characters I could make out from one of the double-columned pages within.

"—the…as much…their…foe as…how…this came…what the…was to…"

There was a particularly striking kanji character that kept popping up, but for some reason, the reading of the character escaped me. It was clear from context that it was a crucial part of the story. It was even printed on the spine of the book.

Nevertheless, I had no idea how to read it.

"……"

With a sense of hopelessness, I lifted my head, then happened to glance over to the side.

A girl was there, reading an old collected edition book with an orange spine.

She was probably about my age. Her hair was short and black, and she had on the kind of dark navy uniform that high school students often wore. Her shirt was buttoned up to the neck, with a crimson ribbon tied at the top. A silver pin shaped like a medieval shield flashed on the collar of her jacket. Her forehead, peeking out from between her bangs, had the intellectual look of a scholar. Maybe this girl would know. I hesitated for a moment but made up my mind and asked her.

"Hey. How do you read this?"

She noticed me and peered at the page of the book I held out toward her, then shifted her round black eyes toward me and gave me a short answer.

"...Whale?"

"Oh, 'whale.' I see."

I nodded to myself. I suddenly remembered that I had read a children's edition of this book in the past (though the title of the book from my childhood, *The Whale*, had "whale" written out phonetically instead of using the kanji character). It may have been by chance, but it made sense to me why I had reached for this particular book.

The girl widened her already big black eyes and looked at me curiously. Her gaze wasn't one of ridicule or suspicion, it was the searching, inquisitive look of an animal biologist observing a newly discovered species. Embarrassed as if she'd seen right through me, I found myself turning my face away. I could feel my heart start to pound louder than usual. I had no idea why I was reacting this way under her stare.

Then suddenly, she shifted her gaze elsewhere.

Wild laughter had erupted from the back of the shelves opposite where we were.

"I totally said so."

"Did you?"

"I dunno."

"Hey, shut up, guys. Hello? It cut out."

Two girls and three guys, all high school–aged, were sitting with their legs up on a reading desk, eating bags of snacks with their cell phones ringing. A silver pin adorned each of their jacket collars. They were students from the same school as the girl.

Elderly library patrons raised their eyebrows in annoyance at the racket they were making.

The girl next to me put her book back on the shelf (the spine of that book—a collection of world literature published by Chikuma Shobo—said *Kafka*), and walked over to them.

The racket paused abruptly.

The long-haired high school girl glared up at her.

"...What?"

"Why don't you go outside if you're going to make a racket?" she asked, keeping her back straight and tall as if summoning her courage.

The other girl with curls and the three guys remained silent, waiting to see what would happen next.

The long-haired girl stood up and looked down at her.

"So we can do whatever we want as long as we go outside?"

"That's for you to decide."

The long-haired girl said nothing for a while, but eventually turned to her friends.

"...Let's go."

They left the building, sniggering quietly.

Over the shelves, I watched her back as she breathed a sigh of relief.

Steady silence once again fell over the library.

But things weren't over for her.

The high school kids from before were lying in wait in the darkness outside the library after hours. The long-haired girl blocked her path and turned to the other girl with the curls, pointing a finger.

"She's been a pain since middle school, and everyone ignores her."

"Really? Then we can do whatever we want to her, yeah?" the girl with the curls suggested condescendingly, jumping on the bandwagon.

"......"

The girl stiffened up and tried to pass by quickly.

"You're not going anywhere." The girls forced her bag away from her and flung its contents all over the ground. Notebooks and pens and the book she had just borrowed (it was the book I had been looking at earlier— *The Kodansha World Literature Collection Volume 15: The Whale*) scattered on the asphalt, as if it was the bully's natural right to do such a thing.

"Stop it."

Their victim attempted to resist for a while, but she was no match for them.

"You said we could do whatever we want as long as we went outside."

"We're not disturbing anybody."

The three guys watched as this went on, laughing.

"Man, you girls are awful."

"Seriously nasty."

"Heh-heh."

Then the three of them noticed something a little ways behind them.

"...Hey."

What they saw was me, standing there motionless as a statue.

Two of the guys stopped laughing for a moment with tense expressions, as if to say, *Crap, we've been caught*, but the one with his hair sticking up turned to me with an affable smile, approaching me apologetically.

"You had to see this, huh? We're just having some issues."

No sooner had he said this, than he rammed his knee into my gut as hard as he could.

"You didn't see anything, right? Right?"

He threatened me in a low voice, as if to say, *You're worthless compared to us. Get out of here. Scram.*

"What's that look for? Got something to say, bitch?"

Seeing that I wasn't putting up a fight, the other two came over, looking relieved.

"Hey, let me have a go at him."

"Me, too."

So saying, they got a laugh out of taking turns kicking my stomach.

As I let them have their way for a while, I was thinking about all the things that had struck me coming back to this city: the emptiness, the distance, the isolation, the unfamiliarity, and the feeling that I had nothing to turn to. And now I thought I had landed on a very small part of what had made me feel that way.

The next moment, I ceased being a statue.

Knocking the three high school guys onto the ground was easier than snapping a twig with my little finger. Leaving them groaning with their hands over their stomachs, the long-haired girl and her friend with the curls fled the scene without saying another word.

I turned to the girl who was cradling her arms and trembling, and our eyes met.

"......"

Not far past the lane from the library was a deserted parking lot. Beyond its green fences was a path leading up to a shrine lined with cherry blossoms, stretching their branches in full bloom. Tiny petals fell noiselessly on the roofs of the parked cars and on the white lines marking the asphalt.

The girl spoke up as she put the notebooks and writing utensils that had been scattered earlier back into her bag.

"They say students at prep schools always get along, but that's such a lie," she said as if to herself, then zipped up her bag carefully and looked at me. "Violence isn't okay. But... Thanks. For saving me."

I was seated on a parking block, flipping through the copy of *The Whale* that she had borrowed.

"I didn't save you."

"Yes, you did."

I pointed at a page and asked, "Hey. How do you read this?"

"......?"

She was confused, and I felt the need to explain somehow.

"I don't know anything. I haven't been to school since elementary school."

Hearing this, she sucked in her breath in disbelief.

"...Honestly?"

"Yeah," I replied and looked back down at the page.

Her face instantly broke out into the gentle smile, and she made an unexpected offer.

"Then I'll teach you all of the characters in that book."

I was up on my feet before I realized, astonished. "...Really?"

She nodded yes, then put her hand on her chest and introduced herself.

"I'm Kaede. That's 'tree' next to 'wind' to write 'Kaede,'" she said, writing her name in the air with a thin finger.

"I'm…"

I hesitated for a moment before saying my name. "I'm Ren. The character for Ren is…"

"Oh, I see. The grass radical and the character for 'sequence'…"

She leaned forward with understanding and once again ran her right finger through the air. Her strokes were precise and accurate. (Just inside the sleeve of her uniform, I caught a glimpse of something like a piece of red string tied around her wrist.)

"Ren."

Kaede called me by my name and smiled.

The tiny petals danced tenderly in the wind.

The twisted alleyways of Jutengai were designed to deter outsiders from wandering in from the human world. The bouquets, flowerpots, and flower baskets placed purposefully in the passages actually served as keys to open the doors that separated the two worlds. After eight long years, I finally understood this mechanism. Understanding it meant I could go between the two cities as I liked.

I started slipping out of Jutengai regularly to visit Shibuya.

But I made sure to keep this a secret from Kumatetsu. I knew that if he found out, he was sure to stop me. I couldn't have that. I had my independence to protect. Slipping away from Kumatetsu was easy. That spring, a huge wave of apprentice prospects flooded Kumatetsu-an for some reason, and he was swamped trying to deal with them all. I told Kumatetsu that I had independently decided to do some training alone in the afternoons and visited Shibuya instead, telling no one.

This was so Kaede could teach me the characters in the book.

I bought the same book for cheap at a used bookstore so that we wouldn't have to borrow the book every time. (I paid for it with my own money, which I had kept for eight years.)

In the red-bricked public library, I would first write out the words and kanji I didn't know into a notebook, then look up their meanings in an elementary school dictionary. Kaede would come by after school, put on her glasses, then check the notebook carefully, giving me practical advice suited to my level like a real teacher.

As I copied the kanji from the book, I felt more and more hopeless. Just how many words did I have to learn in order to read just one book? How much time would I have to spend to do that?

Kaede, who had already finished reading *The Whale*, told me that I didn't have to worry. She explained that this novel was the kind of book that made you want to learn more the further you got into it.

I asked her what she meant by that.

Kaede's reply was this: For example, reading the scene with the multicultural crew makes one want to learn about mid–nineteenth century social history in America, when the book was written (and the history leading up to it). Reading about the ferocious battle against the whale makes one want to look up how whaling was done for whale oil and the history of energy sources after the Industrial Revolution. How did the United States become the world's biggest country after gaining control over the whaling industry? How did Japan, in a state of deliberate isolation until whaling forced open its doors, change in the decades following to become the country it is today? In other words, how does the novel connect to modern times, and what can it tell us about who we are today?

I stopped writing out the kanji in the notebook and listened in awe.

"Right? Makes you want to learn a lot more, doesn't it?" Kaede asked, cocking her head to one side.

I was skeptical if I would ever feel that way.

May came around, and my studying advanced from the elementary level to the middle school level. Kaede provided me with a textbook from her middle school days. Unfortunately, the library didn't allow people to bring in their own books for study. Kaede took me wherever we could find a place to sit, be it the stone steps at a shrine or a park bench or on the grass, and passionately taught me how to learn efficiently in a short period of time. It was all I could do to keep up with her instructions. Kaede seemed determined to teach me all of the subjects.

It wasn't necessarily because I needed a breather from her training, but around that time I was obsessed with looking up anything in the library that concerned the biology of whales. The novel only included written descriptions, and I wanted to look up references that included detailed visual information to cross-check what I had read.

Before I knew it, the rainy season had come, and Kaede started wearing her summer uniform. The navy vest and light blue shirt with its short sleeves went well with her short hair. Her short sleeves now revealed the red string on her wrist prominently. I was wondering aimlessly what kind of meaning that string held for Kaede, when—

"Let's get you some new clothes, too, Ren."

Kaede dragged me to a used clothing store near the station and picked out a few sets of simple jeans and T-shirts. Having grown up in Jutengai, I didn't feel ready to wear the kinds of clothes worn by guys my age in Shibuya. I was reluctant the entire time, but I ended up wearing the jeans and T-shirts that Kaede chose for me anyway. (I paid for them out of my own pocket, obviously.)

Kumatetsu was annoyed that I was gone during the day and apparently harassed Uncle Tata and Uncle Hyaku a few times, yelling, "Where's Kyuta?!" But I ignored all of it. I had more important things to do than spend time with him. I always woke up earlier than Kumatetsu and never failed to do a day's worth of training. He didn't have any right to argue.

July.

"The main character of this novel is seeking revenge against the detestable whale that took his leg. But it seems to me that although it sounds like he's fighting the whale, he's actually fighting himself."

"Himself?"

"I mean, the whale is a mirror in which he sees himself."

"A mirror..."

My textbook had advanced from one for the third year of middle school to one for the first year of high school. Kaede's teaching was on fire. Even as I desperately strived to keep up, I gradually found myself getting drawn in. The books at the library, the writing in the textbooks, Kaede's explanations—everything piqued my curiosity. I had never thought that someone who had spent all of his time training in martial arts could change like this so much. I felt like a new world was opening up. It was fascinating to learn about things I didn't know. And the person who had made me realize this was none other than Kaede.

The rays of early summer made the green row of elms shimmer. The foliage alongside the NHK Hall had recently become the studying spot of choice for Kaede and me.

"Your concentration is amazing. At this rate, you might be able to solve the problems in my study guide in no time at all."

"Only because you're a good teacher, Kaede."

"Really?"

"I'm a little picky when it comes to instructors. Take my word for it."

"By 'instructor,' do you mean that kendo master who raised you?"

It was too difficult to explain everything about myself properly, including Jutengai. So that was how I had explained who Kumatetsu was to Kaede.

"He's a lousy master."

"You really get along with him, don't you?" Kaede laughed.

"No way. We yell at each other all the time."

"Sounds great. I'm jealous."

"Why?"

"Well, to tell you the truth...I've never had a fight with my parents—ever."

"...Huh?"

I looked up from my book.

There was the side of Kaede's face, looking down sadly in a way I had never seen before.

"I exist to make my parents happy. I took entrance exams from when I was in kindergarten and struggled to get the kind of grades they expected me to get, like my life depended on it. But neither of them knows how I feel. They don't even have a clue," she whispered, as if to herself.

I imagined in my head what Kaede's parents must have been like.

Kaede's house was a super-high-rise condominium on the east side of the station, with numerous security guards constantly watching over the spotlessly spacious entrance hall (I had gone up to the entrance once to get a textbook from her). It was obvious that her family must have been very well off. But the girl in front of me didn't look like someone from a house like that. Rather, she looked the same as any kid you might find anywhere, shivering with loneliness. Unable to come up with anything to say, all I could do was keep my mouth shut and listen.

Kaede's eyes now had a look of quiet determination.

"I know, though, that I need to discover who I am for myself, or I'll never be who I really am. That's why, no matter how tough things are now, I need to study as hard as I can so that I can get into university and go live on my own. I'm going to study for my own benefit, become an honor student, do well enough to get a full-tuition scholarship, and graduate all on my own. Then I'll live my own life."

Her head down, Kaede finished talking in a strangled voice.

Suddenly, she lifted her head with a gasp, as if coming out of water to take a deep breath. Then she took a big stretch with an uplifting smile.

"This is the first time I've ever told anyone how I really feel. Wow, I really needed that!"

I thought I saw a hidden fighting spirit behind that gentle face of hers. It was a resolve not to settle for the status quo. I felt like I was starting to see who Kaede really was.

"Hey, about that book."

Kaede smiled at me and went back into her usual teacher mode, then looked down at the copy of *The Whale* in my hands. "I can only teach you so much. There are bound to be teachers who can teach you how to read through that better."

"Where?"

Kaede gave me a sneaky look, then straightened up her back and asked me matter-of-factly:

"Ren, do you have any intention of going to university?"

"What?"

"If you want to apply, I'll help you do it."

"University? But I'm not..."

I was taken aback by the sudden proposal and could only stammer. I really had never even thought of that before.

Kaede's round eyes twinkled daringly as she peered into my face.

"Don't you want to learn a lot more about things you don't know?"

I felt like she was challenging the fighting spirit inside of me.

"...I do."

I choked the words out from between my lips.

Hearing that, Kaede flashed me a bright smile.

"There's a provision called the Upper Secondary School Equivalency Examination. It used to be called the University Entrance Qualification Examination, and it basically qualifies people who haven't graduated from high school to take a university entrance exam..."

Kaede dragged me into the city office the same way she had once dragged me to the used clothing store. After checking the location on the information board, she charged down the hall and sat down with a thump on one of the chairs at the admissions advice counter in the educational affairs division. Kaede explained the situation on my behalf as passionately as if she'd been talking about herself.

But the elderly male employee in charge only opened his mouth to say, "You can't be serious."

Without so much as opening the file of information brochures, he looked sharply at me through his spectacles.

"I don't know what your academic ability is, but if it took you this long to come out of your shell, why don't you start by going to a Public Junior High Night School?"

"But, you see..."

Kaede tried to interject, but the male employee went on without pausing.

"The real world isn't as easy as you think. Even if you do get accepted, how are you going to pay tuition without support from a guardian? Scholarships don't come by easily these days unless you're really exceptional, you know."

Maybe they had a manual for dealing with divergent guys like me who came waltzing in from nowhere.

"No, but…" Kaede still refused to back down.

The male employee took a glance at his watch.

Indignant, Kaede pulled me by the hand and stood up.

"…Fine, I understand!"

Her anger persisted even after returning to the information board.

"What's with that geezer? What a jerk!"

"Look, university's just not meant for me…"

At that moment, a young female employee came running after us with a thick file cradled against her chest. She had been watching our interaction from behind the counter with some concern.

"I'm so sorry about that. You can ask me anything."

She flipped rapidly through the file and spoke all at once. "There are more than a few universities that offer honor student exemptions, and I can direct you to some corporate scholarships that you won't have to pay back. Of course it all depends on your grades, but…," she said as she pulled brochure after brochure out and handed them to us.

Though startled at first, Kaede quickly beamed with her entire face, then bowed to the female employee.

"…Thank you so much!"

I found myself bowing along with her.

"Thank you. Very much…"

I immediately took a look at the Equivalency Exam form. I paled once I saw the page outlining the necessary subject requirements for passing.

"Both math and science are mandatory… I haven't studied those at all."

"You'll do fine, Ren."

"I don't know if I can do this…"

"Leave it to me. I'll make sure you pass, no matter what."

Ding, went the bell for the Residents and Family Registration Division.

The man in charge of the family registration section called us up to the window.

"I understand that you need your residence record in order to take the Equivalency Exam, but it seems that your original record has been removed by the city."

"I knew it..."

I had been away for so long. It was no wonder it was gone.

"However," the man went on, "there was information left in the supplement of your family registry, so we can register a new residence record for you."

The employee pointed at a section of the document, and I became transfixed.

"Please confirm that your father's address written here is correct."

FATHER

"...The father you were separated from?"

Kaede looked up at me with a worried expression.

I briefly explained that I hadn't lived with my dad in over nine years.

"I had no idea where he was. I can't believe I could have found out so easily."

"Are you going to go see him?"

"He might think it's a hassle if I suddenly turn up, or he might have forgotten about me..."

I let out a sad little laugh. Kaede just kept looking at me.

"......"

"But..."

Then again, he might not...

The address indicated a town on the outskirts of Shibuya City. It wasn't the town where the three of us had once lived together, and it wasn't the town where I lived with my mom after that. The name of the town held no memories or familiarity for me.

Alone, I walked there with the address in hand.

I turned away from the road along the Metropolitan Expressway, passed through a narrow shopping street with an intimate air about it, and walked a little ways into a residential area before arriving at the building of the address. This compact apartment complex stood scrunched up in a little spot, tucked away among the rows of giant condominiums in the area.

I looked at my memo again in front of the door. I made sure I wasn't mistaken, then went to knock on the door. But my hand stopped abruptly just before I could.

What do I say? What kind of expression should I make? How do I explain what happened up until now?

I couldn't answer any of those questions. I wasn't prepared at all.

Judging from the laundry out on the balconies of the four-storied apartment complex, it was clear that families occupied most of the rooms. My dad's room was on the very left on the third floor. All that was out on the balcony were a few hangers. It looked as though he could be living alone, but then again, it also looked like he might not be. With the sliding doors closed, I couldn't see inside the room, but it didn't seem like anyone was in there. It was still daytime on a workday. Perhaps it wasn't surprising that no one was home.

Maybe I would leave a letter, or a least a note of some kind.

I sat myself down on one of the blocks in a coin-operated parking lot and took a notebook out of my bag to start writing.

But my pen stopped shortly.

"I have no idea what to write…"

I ended up ripping out the page and crumpling it up.

Then the sudden sound of laughter made me jump, and I looked to where it was coming from.

A kid and his father walked past the parking lot with some mitts and a ball.

"Daddy, give me the ball."

"Ha-ha, there you go."

The kid was about the same age I had been. The father was also about the age I remembered my dad having been.

"……"

After seeing them go off, I looked up at my dad's room once again.

*　　*　　*

Evening was at hand. The other rooms in the apartment complex lit up one by one. Yet nothing changed in my dad's room, and it remained dark.

".⋯.⋯"

Finally giving up, I stood and went back the way I had come, feeling discouraged.

The shopping street at sundown was filled with people. The sun's setting rays reflected against the windows were blinding. Perhaps my dad was somewhere in this crowd. If he lived in that apartment complex, I figured he might buy groceries here on the way from the station.

The dad I remembered was the one from back when he still lived with Mom and me. It had been nine years since then. What was my dad's face like now, what did he do, and what did he look like? Fumbling to come up with a clear image in my mind, I looked for him among the people passing by. Because I kept staring, the men passing by looked at me suspiciously and glared back. In the end, none of them looked like my dad.

I was passing by a shoe store near the end of the shopping street.

A man in a white, short-sleeved shirt with a business bag over his shoulder was crouched in front of the store, tying his shoe. A woman working there came out from the back of the shoe store with an envelope in hand and called out to him.

"Sir, you forgot this."

"Oh."

The man in the shirt lifted his head and stood up.

"You're right. I'm such a klutz."

That voice. I turned back automatically.

The employee handed him the envelope he had left behind. The man in the shirt took it, voicing his appreciation with a kindly smile.

"Thank you."

I couldn't take my eyes off him. My heart was pounding.

Looking down at his envelope, the man in the shirt turned his back to me and started walking away.

I couldn't just let him leave. I firmed my resolve and stepped forward.

"...Excuse me."

The man in the shirt turned his head and looked at me.

"...Yes?"

That face. It really was my dad.

His hair was a little thinner. He had a bit of stubble. But there was no mistaking it. He wasn't a look-alike.

But contrary to what I thought I saw, my confidence was rapidly shriveling up inside me.

The man in the shirt was looking at me as if he had never seen me before.

I put my hand on my chest and asked:

"Do you, by chance...remember me?"

"......"

The man in the shirt seemed not to remember and placed a hand on his head apologetically with an ambiguous smile.

I was speechless.

"I guess not... I'm sorry."

I couldn't bear it. I bowed briefly and left the spot. *Think about it. If he couldn't tell, he might not be my dad, no matter how much he looked like him.*

But then—

"...Ren."

I heard his voice behind me, and I turned back.

"...Ren, is that you?"

The man in the shirt gazed intently at me and said my name in a clear voice.

There was no mistaking it now.

My dad ran over to throw himself at me and embraced me tightly.

"You're all grown-up now... How could I tell?"

I was so stunned in his embrace that I couldn't move. Passersby stared at the two of us standing there giving us strange looks.

My dad spoke in a strangled voice.

"What were you doing all this time...?"

"Oh, well, there was this guy who looked after me, and..."

I stammered out a reply.

"I'm so glad you're safe… I'm so sorry I wasn't able to do anything for you up until now…"

Still hugging me, my dad started crying loudly in the middle of the shopping street, with no regard for who was watching.

"…Dad."

I visited Kaede at school during her lunch break. The compound was off-limits to outsiders, so I told her about the day before through the fence next to the school gate. Kaede seemed relieved.

"Really. That's so great…"

"Apparently, my dad didn't find out about my mom's accident until a lot later. He kept looking for me when he found out I had run away and was missing. For a long time, even after the police gave up."

"I see…"

"Kaede!"

A little ways away, a group of three girls who were probably Kaede's friends pushed one another around as they smiled our way with brimming curiosity.

"Hey, is that your boyfriend, Kaede?"

"He isn't," Kaede said in a flustered voice.

"Then who is he?"

"What school's he from?"

"Leave us alone!"

The trio giggled childishly and went back toward the school building.

Kaede turned to me apologetically. "Sorry."

"It's fine. …But anyway, do you think now I'll get to be normal?"

"Normal?"

"Live with a parent like any normal guy, study and work like normal, and go home and go to bed like normal. Do you think maybe I could live a life like that, too?"

From behind the fence, I looked up at Kaede's high school. The five-story school building had apparently just been renovated and had a section that was glass-paned. Through it, I could see the students enjoying their individual lunch breaks. Girls chatting together. Some guys playing tag. A group of students playing some instruments. Another practicing dance. It was probably nothing special, just an everyday scene that could be found anywhere.

Kaede blinked and spoke as if she could see what I was thinking.

"But you can't decide?"

"……"

"Is this about your master?"

"…Yeah."

"Let me recount what happened to Kyuta and Kumatetsu after that.

"Kyuta returned once the sun had gone down. From the moment he entered the hut, he kept looking at Kumatetsu anxiously. Sensing something dire from his uncharacteristic expression, all Tatara and I could do was look on from the corner of the room.

"Kumatetsu spoke with his back to Kyuta.

"'Where were you off to?'

"'I need to talk to you about something. I want you to listen seriously.'

"'What happened to your training?'

"'Listen. I…'

"'You think it's okay to skip it?'

"'Listen to him, Kumatetsu,' I interjected.

"But perhaps Kumatetsu never intended to listen from the start.

"'Anyway, what the heck is this?' he said, tossing something on the table. It was a math textbook. 'I found this in your bed. I want an explanation.'

"Kyuta stared at it in silence for a while but finally looked up determinedly.

"'…I want to go to a human school.'

" 'What?'

" 'I want to learn about other worlds. So…'

" 'Don't you have other things you need to be doing? I thought you wanted to get stronger.'

" 'I *have* gotten stronger.'

" 'Yeah? Don't make me laugh.'

" 'I'm strong enough now.'

"Kumatetsu stood up abruptly and started ranting, his finger pointed at Kyuta.

" 'What makes you think you're strong, huh?!'

"Kumatetsu's overbearing attitude made Kyuta look at his feet dejectedly, and he spoke, almost to himself.

" '…This always happens whenever I talk to you. You never listen to anything I say and just yell whatever the heck you want.'

" 'Tell me. When did you get stronger?!'

" 'Forget it.'

" 'Wait, where do you think you're going?'

" 'There's something else. …I found my father. That's where I'll go. I just decided.'

" '…What?! You can't be serious…!'

"A crushing sense of shock left Kumatetsu's mouth hanging open, rendering him speechless.

"Kyuta grabbed the textbook and put it into his bag, then left the hut as if to break free from the place.

" '…Hold on. Hey! Don't go!'

"Kumatetsu scrambled desperately down the stone steps and ran in front of Kyuta, blocking his way with arms outstretched. Irritated, Kyuta demanded:

" 'Get out of my way.'

" 'I'm not letting you go!'

"Kumatetsu was trying to stop him by force.

"But Kyuta suddenly grabbed Kumatetsu's collar.

" 'Ack!'

"Before he realized it, Kumatetsu was already in the air. It was a spectacular sweeping hip throw by Kyuta. Helpless, Kumatetsu's body slammed pathetically into the ground with a resounding bang. For a moment, Kyuta looked at that pitiful sight with a pained expression, but he quickly turned his back on Kumatetsu and started to walk off.

"Kumatetsu pushed himself up and yelled in a pleading voice.

"'Don't go, Kyuta! Kyuta!'

"Kyuta didn't look back and continued down the stone steps.

"'Kyuta…!'

"Kumatetsu's voice reached nobody and melted into the darkness of the night.

"A giant summer cumulus cloud stood out magnificently against the bright blue sky. In the front yard of Kumatetsu-an, the fresh-faced apprentices looked timidly mortified during training as Kumatetsu yelled at them.

"'No! No, no, no! Why don't you get it?'

"'I'm sorry.'

"'Anyone with a brain would get it!'

"'I'm sorry.'

"'Stop apologizing for everything!'

"'I'm sorry.'

"'I've had it! Go home!'

"Flinging aside the curtain on his way back into the hut, Kumatetsu ignored Tatara and me in the living room and headed straight for the kitchen, where he gulped down some tap water from a tin cup. Tatara and I exchanged glances at the tension in the air. Tatara looked sick and tired of Kumatetsu's recent irritable behavior.

"'Who would've thought the father would appear after all this time?'

"'Do you suppose he really doesn't mean to come back?'

"'No way he's coming back.'

"'Without Kyuta, Kumatetsu will go back to being a good-for-nothing.'

"'Nah, he's already—'

"Suddenly, Kumatetsu flung the tin cup at us.

"'Shut up!'

"'What the hell? That could have hit us!'

"Tatara sprang up with his fists clenched, but Kumatetsu didn't even look at him and stomped out of the hut in big strides. Kumatetsu stood alone in the front yard, now that the apprentices had left, then sat down with his back hunched.

"Ever since that night, this was how Kumatetsu had been. He vented his irritation on anything and everything, with no regard for the trouble it caused those around him. But I, for one, sympathized with Kumatetsu's frustration then. Despite his flaws, he had thought of himself as something of a parent to Kyuta up until now. He must have been shaken by Kyuta's sudden and unexpected absence and didn't know how to deal with it."

A giant summer cumulus cloud stood out magnificently against the bright blue sky.

"That thing you couldn't decide—Did you figure it out?"

Kaede peered into my face.

"......"

"No, huh?"

I hadn't said anything, yet Kaede guessed the answer.

I honestly couldn't get Kumatetsu out of my head.

I hadn't meant to leave like that. I'd intended to tell him how I honestly felt and ask him what would be the best thing to do. I had wanted him to think about it with me. But it didn't work out that way. The way it turned out was much worse. Maybe I had blown it. I regretted what happened. But I couldn't go back to the way things were anymore.

"It doesn't matter anymore," I said, brushing it off. "I'm about to go meet with my dad now. Then everything will work itself out."

"Are you sure you aren't just toughing it out?"

"Why would I do that?"

"I'll be at the library all day today. Come find me if you need me."

Kaede saw me off with concern in her eyes.

"...Ren!"

Come evening, my dad was waiting for me in the crowded shopping street. As soon as he saw me, he raised his hand with his bag dangling off of his shoulder and gave me a cheery smile.

I couldn't return his smile with my own.

He lifted the grocery store bag in his hand for me to see.

"Omelet with ham for dinner tonight. Let's make it and eat together."

Omelet with ham had been my favorite dish as a kid.

"Sure."

I reluctantly forced myself to smile.

My dad kept on talking on the way back to the apartment complex with his bicycle in tow. I shuffled along behind him with my head down. He didn't talk about the past and instead focused on random, innocuous things that had happened recently, as if in a strained effort to fill the silence. I quietly listened to him talking, without chiming in.

When my dad brought the subject up, he did so carefully as if to gauge the situation.

"...By the way, could you tell me a bit more about this person who took care of you all this time?"

"Huh?"

"I need to meet him and thank him properly. Then we'll start living together."

"...Hold on."

Startled, I stopped my feet unconsciously.

My dad stopped pushing his bicycle and turned back toward me.

"What...? It's only proper."

"I mean..."

Explaining where I had been and what kind of life I had led until now to my dad was a very difficult issue. That's why I had only told him that there was a person who had taken care of me. Who could blame him for wanting to know more?

Still, I wasn't close enough with my dad yet to tell him everything. We had lived apart from each other for nine whole years.

"I mean…I can't get over the time we spent apart just like that."

"…I see. Sorry," my dad said apologetically. "Of course you can't. Kids don't experience time the same way adults do. To me, the time I spent with you and Mom seems like it was just yesterday."

"Yesterday…"

Shocked by the sheer gap between our perceptions, I was rendered speechless.

"Sorry I rushed you," my dad said, scanning the sky with his gentle smile. "Let's start over a little bit at a time. So you can forget all the unhappiness you've had so far and look forward…"

Suddenly, something writhed inside my chest. That something immediately took over my entire body and transformed itself into a hostile urge. I confronted my dad in a low, sharp voice.

"Start what over?"

"What?"

My dad turned around, surprised at my sudden change.

"Why would you assume that I was unhappy? What do you know about me?"

"Ren."

"Don't talk like you understand when you don't know me at all!"

"Ren, I…"

At that moment, a burst of oblivious laughter passed by my dad and me. It was a group of high school guys cycling past, on the way home from club practice. My rant was cut short, and my aggression shriveled rapidly. With nowhere to go, what rage I had left came out as words directed at myself.

"…Of course you don't know. I haven't told you anything. …Sorry. I think it's better if we cancel today."

Unable to bear it, I broke away and turned my back on my dad, walking away.

"Ren, it's up to you to decide what you want to do from here. But…!"

My dad's voice pierced me from behind. "But just remember. If there's anything I can do, I'll do it with all my power. So, please!"

I walked forcefully though the city as darkness fell across it.

"…What's wrong with me? What do I want? Why would I say something like that to my dad?"

What was the thing that had writhed inside my chest back there? My mind was a mess. I didn't understand myself. Needing to escape, I walked quickly as if to run away.

Suddenly, a voice rang out in my head.

Don't go!

It was Kumatetsu.

I shook my head.

"Damn it! Why am I thinking of him?"

My dad's kind face spoke softly.

Let's start over.

I shook my head.

"Damn it!"

Kumatetsu yelled again.

Don't go!

Then where was I supposed to go?

"Damn it, damn it, damn it! I don't know!"

I couldn't stop myself from running.

I had somehow returned to the bustling center of Shibuya.

Panting heavily, I stopped and caught my breath, with my hands on my knees. The city was teeming with people as always. Everyone passing by looked happy. I had to be the only one with my head down in a lively place like this.

A sign flashed in front of the building across the road. I noticed that something was slowly twisting and emerging in the light of the sign.

"......?"

The twisting seemed to focus into an image and eventually formed itself into a clear figure.

i hate you... i hate you...

I gulped.

"......?"

i hate you... i hate you...

It was the shadow of a small child.

"That's...me, when I was little..."

I remembered. It was the shadow I had left behind there nine years earlier, when I had run away from the relatives from the head family. The shadow seemed to want to say something and slowly turned to face me. That's when I saw the large gaping hole in its chest.

"...A hole? What is that...?"

The small shadow smirked. Then suddenly—

"Huh...?"

It vanished without a trace.

I looked around in alarm. But all I could see were the waves of people going up and down the slope, and it was nowhere to be seen. Where was it? Where had it gone?

It hadn't disappeared.

The shadow had moved around behind me.

"?!"

I turned to find a mirror displayed in the building behind me, and instead of my reflection, there was my shadow, smirking. The gaping hole swirled in its chest.

The hole was hollow and bottomless.

"...What is this...?"

Shaken, I clutched my chest. Of course there was no hole. But the huge hole in my shadow before me was undeniably there. As if to clearly indicate a defect. I grabbed wildly at my chest, feeling as though I would go insane as I looked at the shadow. Grinning eerily, the shade insistently flaunted its empty hole at me. I was about to explode.

"Aaaaaargh!"

Letting out a yell, I started running as if to escape.

The lights were already out when I arrived in front of the library. Only the outside notice board gave off its cold fluorescent light. My body was utterly exhausted from running, and I slumped onto the closed gate and tried to open it by force.

The gate wouldn't budge.

Kaede must have gone home by now. Of course she would have, now that the library was closed. I gave up and let my hand drop. Where should I go from here? I didn't have anywhere to go.

"...Ren?"

I heard a voice.

Beyond the light of the notice board stood Kaede, her bag held to her chest.

"Your face is so menacing right now. It's almost like it's not you," Kaede said, looking at me. We were in the parking lot next to the shrine where we had sat once before.

I couldn't look at Kaede properly because of the choking feeling in my chest. I kept my hands on my face and glared at her through my fingers.

"...Tell me. What am I, exactly? A human? Or a beast?"

"A beast?"

"Or some hideous monster?"

"What are you talking about?"

Kaede looked at me closely, as if trying to see into my shadowy darkness.

"Tell me. Please. Am I..."

With my face covered, I stumbled over to Kaede, my steps uncertain. Kaede clutched her bag firmly to her chest to guard herself and backed warily away. Not about to let her escape, I loomed over her with outstretched arms. The wire fence of the parking lot shook violently with a heavy clang.

Pressing her entire back against the wire fence, Kaede trembled as she spoke.

"Ren, you're not acting normally…"

"What am I…?! What…!"

I closed in on Kaede, snarling.

"……!"

Kaede glared at the shadowy darkness with a determined look and slapped me hard in the face as if to drive it away.

The blow stunned me. I didn't know what had happened. All of my energy drained from my body, and I felt like I would collapse on the spot as I reeled backward. Kaede hastily leaned up and wrapped her arms around my neck to draw me toward her, and the two of us slumped into the wire fence. Kaede kept holding on to me tight as if to keep me from something.

"There are times when I feel so awful I don't know what to do, too. I don't care what happens anymore, and I feel like something's going to burst out from inside. It's not just you, Ren, and it's not just me. I'm sure everyone gets that. So it's okay… It's okay."

Kaede whispered as if telling herself the same thing and closed her eyes.

Cradled in Kaede's arms, I felt the choking sensation in my chest dissipating. I found that I could finally lift my face.

I faced Kaede and looked into her round eyes properly.

"Thanks. I'm better now. I'll cool my head and think about it some more."

Kaede smiled with relief and said that she was glad to see the Ren she knew again. Then she suddenly thought of something and set her fingers on her right wrist.

She was untying the piece of red string.

"Here. It's the bookmark from my favorite book when I was little. It's saved me a lot."

Kaede drew my right hand toward her and tied it onto my wrist, then pressed me to make a promise with her.

"If you're ever worried about yourself or feel like you did just now, remember this."

I stared at the bookmark she had tied around my wrist for me.

"A good-luck charm," Kaede said.

When I returned to Jutengai, I was in for a surprise.

Elaborate decorations were set up all over the city—on the gate with the neon signs, on the water tower, and on the trees lining the river. It was like a carnival had come to town.

"...What is this? What's going on?"

Bewildered, I looked around this way and that. A huge lantern in the square had the silhouettes of Kumatetsu and Iozen painted on it. Could this mean...?

"Kyuta!"

Hearing my name, I turned to find Jiromaru there, grinning from ear to ear.

"Why don't you stop by my place?"

Jiromaru's home—in other words, Iozen's home—stood on prime property on the hill to the east of Jutengai.

Large sliding doors painted with boars and bamboo adorned the tatami room, which was as spacious as a museum. No other mansion was as expansive as this, the only exception being the grandmaster's hermitage.

Despite living in such an extravagant home, Jiromaru was an unpretentious, informal individual. We relaxed on the ceramic stools set in front of the veranda, just as we had always done since we were kids, and had a leisurely chat. We gazed out at the well-maintained bamboo forest in the yard as we drank the tea Jiromaru's mother brought us and munched on some snacks.

"The grandmaster announced the date so suddenly, the whole town's scrambling to make preparations."

"The date?"

"Tomorrow is the day my pops and your master fight it out. The match to decide who the new grandmaster will be…" Jiromaru's eyes widened. "Don't tell me you didn't know?"

I turned my face down a little as I spoke. "We had a bit of a fight, actually. Things got awkward, and I haven't seen him in a while."

"I see… But I haven't seen my pops, either. He's been really busy training. It's a little sad, but what can I do? I want my pops to win. You wouldn't want your master to lose, either, would you? Then forget the awkwardness and go cheer him on," Jiromaru said, trying to cheer me up.

"…Yeah."

"Whoever wins, we'll still be friends."

Standing up, Jiromaru smiled cheerily and held out his right hand. His eyes were clear and straightforward. I stood up to return his handshake.

"Of course."

"Let's hope it'll be a good fight."

"Yeah."

We regarded each other and smiled.

"Jiromaru."

We looked toward the voice to find Ichirohiko standing between the open sliding doors. He had shown up at some point, and was watching us fondly.

"Brother," Jiromaru responded with a smile.

Ichirohiko looked at his younger brother with amazingly kind eyes.

"You mustn't keep Kyuta for too long. Come, it's evening already. I'll see him off to the front gate."

The evening cicadas were buzzing in the yard.

I walked through the empty bamboo forest with Ichirohiko. As always, Ichirohiko had his mouth hidden behind the scarf wrapped around his neck.

It felt odd to have him see me off. Things had been different when we were little, but recently we'd hardly had the opportunity to talk. Since he had offered to see me off himself, I assumed that he wanted to speak to me about something. I mentally prepared myself for all sorts of questions I thought he might ask, but Ichirohiko didn't say anything in the end, and I was left hanging.

Once we got up to the small gate, I turned back toward Ichirohiko. "Thanks. Well, then…"

Just then, a shard of bamboo suddenly whizzed by me, grazing my cheek.

"Ow…!"

What was that just now?

I recoiled, and Ichirohiko's fist flew at me as if he had been waiting for that moment.

"Huh?"

Taken by surprise, I took a clean hit to the stomach.

I didn't even have time to ask why before collapsing on the ground.

The glint in Ichirohiko's eyes right then was too dreadful to describe. With evident hatred, he kicked me persistently, again and again.

"What do you mean…'a good fight'? Don't make me laugh. …You, a human…and Kumatetsu, too… You should know your place…like the outcasts that you are…!"

This was the first I had ever seen Ichirohiko like this. I had never imagined that the star student from our childhood could have been concealing such a violent side. Completely at his mercy and unable to resist, I just endured the pain.

Eventually, Ichirohiko stopped kicking me, apparently satisfied. The shards of bamboo that had been floating in the air scattered onto the ground.

"…Remember that."

That's when I saw it.

The black hole in Ichirohiko's chest as he went to leave.

It was the same hole I had in my chest.

A hole… What…? Ichirohiko…has the same hole I have… Why?

The call of the evening cicadas echoed emptily through the bamboo forest.

THE COLISEUM

"That day, the beasts in Jutengai all swarmed the coliseum.

"Finally, the day had come for Kumatetsu and Iozen to settle things once and for all.

"That meant it was also the day to decide who would become the new grandmaster.

"The cloudless summer sky peered in from the giant hole in the coliseum's canopy. True to Jutengai's reputation as a city of textiles, beneath the canopy hung countless giant sheets of cloth in a myriad of colors, adding flair to the grand occasion. The seats, with a capacity of nearly fifty thousand, were suffused with elated enthusiasm, and by midday, it was completely packed with no space to move. All kinds of voices echoed from every direction, amid the vendors calling out to sell their drinks and snacks.

"'I'm for Iozen.'

"'I think it'll be Kumatetsu.'

"'Kumatetsu will win.'

"'No, it'll be Iozen.'

"'Of course Iozen will win.'

"'Well, it might just end up being Kumatetsu.'

"Children, the elderly, women, men, the rich, craftsmen—beasts of all types sat in the same seats indiscriminately, gazing at the circular arena in the middle of the coliseum and voicing their personal predictions. It was clear just how much they had all looked forward to this day.

"The usual gamble-loving trio was there off to the side of the seats teeming with beasts, leaning their heads in and furtively placing their bets.

"'I say Iozen.'

"'I say Kumatetsu.'

"'I say… Dang, I can't decide!'

"The grandmaster made a speech, dressed in a particularly elaborate robe with ceremonious embroidery.

"'I thought about it long and hard! I pondered what kind of god I wanted to be when I join the ranks of the divine. For nine years, I pondered and pondered and pondered some more!' he joked with some exaggeration, then passed his gaze over the spectators. 'But at long last, I have come to a decision.'

"A homely-looking youngster with a bearded face stood up from his seat and spoke up.

"'And what kind of god are ya gonna be?'

"The grandmaster answered.

"'A god of decisiveness, of course.'

"Laughter erupted throughout the venue. Everyone wished to congratulate the grandmaster on his retirement, and that naturally led to a storm of applause. It was a testament to just how much everyone loved him.

"'After the match, I shall perform the reincarnation rites with help from the other sages, so you can all look forward to that.'

"So saying, the grandmaster returned to his seat.

"The head referee called out in a deep voice that rang through every corner of the coliseum:

"'Starting now, we shall begin the ritual to decide Jutengai's new grandmaster! Candidates, step forward!'

"With a great roar, an earth-shaking cheer exploded from the crowd.

"I could see a cloaked Iozen make his entrance from the west gate. Ichirohiko and the sword-bearing Jiromaru were just behind him, and they were further followed by his tough-looking apprentices, all wearing matching jackets.

"Then from the east gate came our boy Kumatetsu.

"Hyakushubo and I walked behind him. Kumatetsu-an's fresh-faced apprentices trailed along after us. Evidently overwhelmed by the scale of the venue, they all kept looking around nervously with their mouths hanging open.

"I compared our posse with Iozen's.

"'Wow, we clearly look worse off just by the apprentices' faces.'

"'If only Kyuta were here,' Hyakushubo muttered in complaint. That went without saying. If Kyuta had been there, we wouldn't have let some pimple-faced rookie act as sword-bearer.

"Kumatetsu's head hung low the whole time, and he wore a sullen expression. He had been that way ever since the night Kyuta had left. He really was a hopeless bastard. I glared at him impatiently.

"'What's with the glum face, man? The match's about to start. I hope you know that.'

"Kumatetsu suddenly stopped and shook his head violently, then let out a sudden roar as if to shake off his hesitation.

"'Raaaaaaaaaaaaaaar!'

"Startled by that absurdly deafening voice, we all put our hands over our ears.

"'Whoa, not so loud, idiot!'

"Iozen saw this and grinned, then let out his own roar as if to answer Kumatetsu's.

"'Raaaaaaaaaaaaaaar!'

"As the two began their howling match, the onlooking beasts stood up one by one to let out their own howls.

"Countless wild howls spread like a wave, eventually encompassing the entire coliseum.

"Among these spectators was Kyuta, hiding with a hood covering his head, but neither Kumatetsu nor we had any idea about that yet.

"The start of the match was drawing closer by the minute."

*   *   *

"I gazed intently at Iozen and Kumatetsu as they faced each other in the central arena of the coliseum.

"Iozen was decked out with elaborate festive feather decorations on his shoulders and spiked arm protectors of tanned leather, with a twisted ceremonial rope tied around his waist in place of a sash. He took his jet-black sword, with its hand guard and scabbard tied together, and slowly stuck it in place at his waist.

"Across from him, Kumatetsu had a cloth dyed with sun emblems wrapped around his shoulders. His tanned leather protectors and twisted rope were the same as Iozen's. He prepared himself by slinging the great sword with its crimson scabbard over his shoulder.

"The apprentices on either contestant's side took their positions in the official seats near the east and west gates respectively. From Kumatetsu's section on the east side, the fresh-faced apprentices, Tatara, and I looked on with tense expressions.

"The grandmaster sat on a lavish chair in the special seating section, looking down with a peaceful smile. The guest sages could be seen on either side of him. Among them were the baboon, the long-haired cat, and the seal we had met before on our journey.

"The head referee's voice rang out.

"'According to custom, your swords must remain sheathed. Drawing them is forbidden. You admit defeat if you flee. You also lose if you are knocked out for ten seconds. You must respect all other conventional formalities and rules.'

"Flags of the various districts of Jutengai fluttered behind the referee seats. This indicated that the referees were composed of representatives from each district. There were two additional assistant referees, and the head referee sat in the center. All of the officiates wore brightly striped traditional noblemen's attire in black and orange, complete with traditional headgear.

"'Ready yourselves!'

"Kumatetsu held his arms out and lowered himself into a fighting stance.

"Iozen remained upright and purposefully gripped the hilt of his sword.

"The beasts watched with bated breath.

"The entire coliseum was masked in silence.

"Then—

"'Begin!'

"The match started with the head referee's call.

"Instantly, Kumatetsu made a sharp charge at Iozen. His sword swayed violently from side to side. Iozen prepared for him, lowering his stance.

"'Raaaaaaaaaaaar!'

"Just before he got to Iozen, Kumatetsu suddenly let his fur bulge out in a surprise maneuver and transformed into his beast form. His muscles expanded, and the protectors on his forearms and back were blown off with a loud snap.

"'Oh come on, right from the start?!' Tatara yelled.

"Iozen caught Kumatetsu's first blow with his right arm. But Kumatetsu's massive body blasted that arm aside, and he doled out his second and third blows one right after the other. Iozen evaded them by stepping back and swaying, but he was unable to dodge Kumatetsu's left cross punch that followed and blocked it instead.

"Kumatetsu's intense barrage of strikes had Iozen completely on the defensive.

"'Kumatetsu has the upper hand?!'

"I hadn't expected this. The apprentices voiced their joy, seeing Kumatetsu in the lead.

"But Tatara mumbled with evident concern:

"'That idiot, he's not pacing himself at all...'

"'Yaaaagh!'

"Kumatetsu thrust forth his right fist with all his might.

"Iozen blocked the strike with his arms crossed, but the force blew his body backward, slamming him into the wall of the arena.

"'Pops!'

"Jiromaru called out in concern from the official seating area.

"Ichirohiko turned to his brother next to him and yelled irritably:

"'Quiet. Just watch!'

"In the billowing clouds of dirt, Iozen could be seen calmly drawing his sword, sheath and all. He didn't appear to have received any damage at all.

"Kumatetsu rushed at him on all fours to follow up on his attack.

"Gracefully coming to a stop, Iozen unexpectedly readied his sword *en garde* like a fencer. Astonished murmurs broke out among the spectators. They had never seen anyone wield a katana in such a way.

"Kumatetsu's colossal body swayed as he stampeded forward, and Iozen evaded him at the very last second like a matador. He was prepared for the next rush at him as well, and the two just missed each other by a hair. Iozen seemed to be gauging his timing precisely. For Kumatetsu's third rush at him, Iozen evaded with an acrobatic flip and even made a spectacular landing.

"The coliseum erupted with a massive roar of cheering and applause. In one fell swoop, Iozen's performance had shifted the venue's mood in his favor.

"'You see?' Ichirohiko exclaimed proudly.

"As if to declare that the fun was over, Iozen flicked his sword through the air to clear the cloud of dirt, then lowered his stance and made a sharp rush for his opponent. Meanwhile, Kumatetsu repeatedly charged forward blindly like a slow-witted creature.

"The two collided in the center of the coliseum.

"With a heavy crash, a huge cloud of dirt rose up. Iozen could be seen spinning his body back and repositioning his stance. Shifting one's gaze to the other side revealed Kumatetsu back down to his regular size, flat on the ground amid a great dust cloud.

"'Ooh!'

"We held our heads in our hands, covered our eyes, and cried out.

"'Uurgg... Damn it!'

"Kumatetsu shook his head out on all fours. It was clear to everyone that he had sustained significant damage.

"Then something raged toward him, shaking the ground with a thunderous rumble and clearing the dirt clouds in its path.

"It was Iozen, transformed into an enormous boar beast.

"'Crap!'

"Kumatetsu stood up quickly but wasn't quick enough to stop the boar from ramming into him head-on. The impact smacked the blade on his back, sending it far across the arena.

"'Damn!'

"Kumatetsu hastily started running to retrieve it.

"But Iozen wasn't about to let him. He rushed in front of Kumatetsu to obstruct his way and blew heavily out of his big snout threateningly.

"Kumatetsu was stuck with his path blocked off.

"Next to an elated Jiromaru, Ichirohiko watched with confidence.

"'That's only to be expected of Father.'

"The enormous boar charged forward and whacked Kumatetsu violently into the air—not once, but twice. Not just twice, but a third time again. Kumatetsu was being thrashed easily. It was hard to believe now that he ever had the upper hand.

"'This ain't good.'

"Tatara propped one knee up and bit his finger in agitation.

"I was pale. 'The fool. He's getting trounced.'

"The enormous boar was overwhelming the staggered Kumatetsu and mercilessly piled on the attacks.

"Even the sages in the special seating section seemed to consider the outcome clear.

"'Now, this…'

"'Perhaps this is it.'

"The grandmaster simply watched without saying a word.

"Kumatetsu kept getting battered about with no means to resist. He was rapidly accumulating bruises all over his body. He hardly seemed able to stay upright anymore.

"Tatara appeared exasperated beyond measure. He shot up onto his feet and hollered, 'Don't tell me this is it, Kumatetsu!' while shaking his fist in the air.

"But a split second later, Iozen blasted Kumatetsu high into the air like some piece of rubbish.

"It was a decisive blow.

"Kumatetsu slowly sailed through the air and fell brutally to the ground.

"With a roar, the onlooking beasts rose to their feet one by one. Some raised their arms in triumph, some buried their heads in their arms, some put on jubilant smiles, and some watched worriedly with hands over their mouths...

"'One!'

"The head referee started his count.

"Kumatetsu was splayed out and didn't so much as twitch.

"'Two! Three!'

"Whoever got knocked out for a ten-count would lose.

"'Four! Five!'

"The referees from each district stood up one by one in order to witness the outcome.

"'Six! Seven!'

"Kumatetsu remained unconscious.

"'Eight!'

"Just then, a man leaned out from the very front row near the east gate.

"'Kyuta?!'

"Jiromaru cried out, recognizing him.

"That moment, Kumatetsu's body jerked forcefully. He had regained consciousness.

"Just before the count of nine, the head referee stopped his count.

"The figure standing atop the railing before the front row was indeed Kyuta.

"A murmur broke out among the beasts.

"'It's Kyuta.'

"'Did he say Kyuta?'

"'It's Kumatetsu's head apprentice, Kyuta.'

"Much to our surprise, Kyuta was in the coliseum. He had been watching Kumatetsu's match this whole time. No doubt he had seen Kumatetsu losing and couldn't help but show himself.

"'Urg... Urrg...'

"Although Kumatetsu had come to, he was still lying facedown, gasping painfully and unable to get up.

"I suddenly came to my senses and yelled out beseechingly toward Kyuta:

"'Kyuta, please! Give Kumatetsu some encouragement!'

"I reckoned the only thing that could give Kumatetsu a boost in this situation was Kyuta cheering him on.

"But instead, Kyuta took a deep breath and, looking down at Kumatetsu, hollered as loudly as he possibly could:

"'What are you doing, you moron?!'

"His voice was full of reproach, about as far from encouragement as it could get.

"'Stand up already!'

"But Kumatetsu opened his eyes when he heard that voice. He bore the pain from his injuries and struggled to get up.

"'...Hey, you've got some nerve, showing your face here after you up and left...'

"'And why are you looking so pathetic?! You oughta be ashamed!'

"'...What did you say, you little twerp...?'

"I looked back and forth between the two of them, my face pale.

"'This is no time to be squabbling at each other!'

"'Are you kidding me? Why are those two always like this?' Tatara muttered with his head in his hands.

"Yet Kyuta remained strong and unwavering as he continued berating Kumatetsu.

"'What's with the mopey face?! So you're on your own—hurry up and win already!'

"'...Ha. I didn't need you sticking your nose in. I wasn't going to lose any...way!'

"And with that, the impossible happened.

"Kumatetsu suddenly snapped himself up. And with so much force that his entire body sprang into the air.

"'Graaaaaaaar!'

"His howl echoed through the whole of the coliseum. It was a cry that indicated Kumatetsu was back on his feet.

"'......?'

"Iozen, who had started his walk back to the west gate, turned around at the roar.

"Kumatetsu landed with a thud and immediately made a furious dash toward his sword lying on the ground.

"Realizing what was happening, Iozen started running to stop him.

"Kumatetsu sprinted madly toward his weapon like a wild monkey.

"'*Raaaaaagh!*'

"But Iozen got to the blade a step ahead. He readied his sword and stood in the way, determined to stop Kumatetsu from passing.

"However—

"'?!'

"Before Iozen even had a chance to see, Kumatetsu smoothly slipped by his side and slid on the ground to grab his sword.

"Seeing Kumatetsu completely back in the game, the venue shook with a roar of awestruck approval. Tatara and I could only stare blankly in weary disbelief. Those two simply defied our understanding.

"The sages in the special seating section voiced their admiration.

"'To think he's still keen to fight.'

"'Now this is getting interesting.'

"The grandmaster responded with a happy smile.

"Kumatetsu readied his great sword in front of him and slid it downward as he went for Iozen. As he did so, Iozen repositioned his own sword up high from his midsection and went for Kumatetsu.

"The two scabbards clashed fiercely together in the center of the coliseum with a reverberating zing.

"They were evenly matched.

"Kyuta yelled fervidly from the east gate:

"'Coming in from the right! Sway! Counterattack!'

"As if following Kyuta's directions, Kumatetsu swayed to evade a strike to his midsection from the right and went for the counterattack.

"'You've got this! Get his midsection!' Kyuta continued to yell.

"Neither budging an inch, their furious exchange continued. It was such an intense clash of swords that steam rose up off Kumatetsu's body.

"Tatara and I were baffled by Kumatetsu's expression.

"'...Look at the bastard's face. He's smiling.'

"'It's the face he makes when he's training with Kyuta.'

"'Can't be. He's in the middle of a match.'

"'He must be so happy to have Kyuta back.'

"Kumatetsu lunged with his sword, that smile still on his face.

"The baboon sage sounded impressed.

"'His heart is now somewhere beyond his opponent. Truly a state of complete concentration, of utter selflessness.'

"'Kumatetsu alone could never hope to win,' the grandmaster said assertively, then added with a glance at Kyuta, 'But with the two of them, who knows?'

"Kumatetsu doled out strike after strike with his sword, and the tables were gradually turning.

"A concerned-looking Jiromaru pressed his hands together and whispered in prayer:

"'Come on, Pops!'

"Iozen recoiled from a concentrated blow from Kumatetsu and just managed to meet it with his hand guard, but he was being pushed back bit by bit. Anyone could see that Iozen was struggling now.

"'No! He's going to lose!'

"Jiromaru cried out loud without thinking.

"Suddenly—

"'Ack!'

"Somebody hit him with enough force to slam his face in, toppling Jiromaru over.

"'Hold your tongue!'

"It was an infuriated Ichirohiko who had struck him down. 'Father would never lose to the likes of Kumatetsu! Ever!'

"'...Brother...?'

"Jiromaru was stunned by Ichirohiko's sudden change.

"'Kyuta...!'

"Ichirohiko turned his glare on Kyuta with ever-increasing hatred.

"But Kyuta didn't even notice. He simply continued to call out to Kumatetsu.

"'That *human*! He's got some nerve...!'

"Ichirohiko's hatred deepened even more.

"'Graaaaar!'

"Iozen let out a determined roar and turned to the offensive, pushing Kumatetsu back with the guard of his sword. Their hand guards clashed, and the swords creaked against each other dangerously.

"'Urg...'

"Kumatetsu's face contorted under the strain of being repelled.

"'Don't let him overpower you! Don't let him get the better of you!' Kyuta shouted, with his fists clenched tight. 'Use that ridiculous power of yours!'

"'Agggh!'

"Sweat spewed out of Kumatetsu. Though struggling, he managed to hold his ground.

"'Raah!'

"He pushed the hand guard back with all of his might.

"Kumatetsu held his sword in front of his body.

"Iozen held his own above his head.

"The two swords collided sharply together.

"Their scabbards vibrated fiercely against each other with a reverberating hum.

"With a snap, a small crack appeared on Iozen's black scabbard. As we watched, the crack spread rapidly across the entire scabbard.

"After a short pause, it shattered all at once, leaving only the bare blade.

"'Now!'

"Kyuta cried out sharply, and Kumatetsu responded by twisting his body and throwing aside the sword in his hand.

"'What?!'

"Iozen failed to grasp his opponent's intent.

"Planting a hand on the ground for support, Kumatetsu landed a flying kick to Iozen's hand, still holding the sword.

"The blade flew from Iozen's grasp and up into the special seating section, barely missing the grandmaster and plunging into the back of his lavish chair.

"'Eeek!' the grandmaster cried out.

"As Iozen recoiled, Kumatetsu put his whole force behind a fist aimed at the boar's cheek.

"Iozen also struck out with his fist, but he was a second too late.

"'Raaaaar!'

"Sweat flew up like the spray from a wave.

"Kumatetsu's fist slammed squarely into Iozen's face.

"'......!'

"A hush fell over the coliseum.

"Having received the full brunt of the blow, Iozen staggered a few steps, trying to keep himself upright, but failed, and collapsed like a log.

"The head referee's voice rang out:

"'One! Two!'

"Everyone was speechless, unable to move.

"'Three! Four!'

"Jiromaru and Iozen's apprentices, of course.

"'Five! Six!'

"But Tatara and the fresh-faced apprentices as well.

"'Seven! Eight!'

"No one looking on dared to move.

"'Nine! Ten!'

"And finally…the head referee raised all ten of his fingers.

"'We have a winner: Kumatetsu!'

"The moment he declared this, the coliseum exploded in thunderous applause. So much celebratory confetti fluttered through the air that we could hardly see in front of us. Every face in the audience beamed with satisfaction. It didn't matter if they had been rooting for Iozen or Kumatetsu; their smiles simply expressed contentment at having witnessed an excellent match.

"Wounded all over his body, Kumatetsu turned around and slowly walked toward Kyuta. Kyuta stepped off the railing, back down to the seats to greet Kumatetsu. Kumatetsu stopped in front of Kyuta.

"Kyuta looked straight at his master and spoke softly:

"'Don't scare me like that.'

"'Who asked you to worry?'

"'I can't believe you managed to win.'

"'Of course I was gonna win.'

"'Yeah, right. You were totally worn out.'

"'Shaddup.'

"Kyuta lifted his arm and held his palm up.

"Kumatetsu also lifted his arm and held his palm up.

"The two palms came together with a sharp slap.

"Kyuta looked at Kumatetsu with affection, and Kumatetsu looked at Kyuta with pride. I watched this scene unfold with disbelief. Kumatetsu and Kyuta, who had done nothing but bicker at each other from the day they had met, had reached a point of high-fiving each other as if to confirm their mutual trust. A satisfied chuckle escaped Kumatetsu's mouth. The grin on his face was straightforward and sincere. I imagine that it came not from winning the match or gaining the title of grandmaster, but from the satisfaction of having fought as one with Kyuta.

"'It's the birth of a new grandmaster!'

"Unrestrained applause erupted from the spectators.

"Iozen was now sitting up, regarding the two of them gently.

"'...A good son, that boy is.'

"The apprentice next to him failed to hear and asked, 'What was that?' But Iozen didn't answer and called out to his other apprentices in the arena to get ready to go.

"'Ho-ho.'

"The grandmaster seemed pleased about the whole thing.

"Then he turned, looking at the back of his seat, and realized something.

"'Iozen's sword that was sticking out a minute ago… It's gone?'

"The grandmaster snapped his head back toward the arena.

"There, he saw something moving rapidly among the confetti.

"That something was Iozen's sword.

"A dull thunk resounded through the arena.

"'…Huh?'

"Kyuta had no idea what had just happened.

"Kumatetsu's hand fell away from his.

"As Kumatetsu staggered backward unsteadily, raw spots of red seeped into the ground near his feet. Kumatetsu looked down at them in a daze and groaned.

"'What's all this red stuff…? Eh…? Kyuta, what's going on?'

"He looked to Kyuta as if asking for help.

"The sword had pierced Kumatetsu's back.

"At that moment, a sudden cry of laughter rang out in the hushed coliseum.

"'Ha-ha-ha-ha-ha-ha!'

"Iozen snapped his head back toward the official seating area.

"'?!'

"There stood Ichirohiko, holding out his left hand.

"'Father! I have settled the match with my telekinesis and your sword. Victory is yours! You would never lose to an outcast like Kumatetsu, after all!' he said, smiling proudly at Iozen.

"Smiling—yes. Ichirohiko's mouth, which he had kept concealed all this time, showed from under the loosened cloth, revealing his face to all the beasts in the coliseum. He was missing the boar tusks that Iozen and Jiromaru had, as well as the long snout. His face was clearly that of a human.

"'Isn't that right, Kyuta… Isn't it?!'

"Ichirohiko glared at Kyuta with crazed eyes, and an eerie, shadowy darkness materialized on his chest.

"'Wh-what the hell is that…?!' Tatara rasped out in alarm.

"'…A hole?' I whispered. What was there could only be described as a hole in the middle of his chest.

"Then a shadowy darkness in the shape of a hand appeared on the hilt of the sword stuck in Kumatetsu's back.

"'D-don't do it, Ichirohiko!'

"Iozen rushed to stop Ichirohiko. It seemed he already knew something and feared it. Ichirohiko smiled at the frantic Iozen.

"'Father. I shall finish him off now. Watch.'

"Ichirohiko pushed his left hand forward, and the hand-shaped shadow pushed the sword deeper, as if controlled from a distance.

"Kumatetsu staggered and fell to his knees on the arena floor scattered with confetti and slumped forward.

"'……!'

"Kyuta could do nothing but stare at what was happening with his mouth agape.

"Ichirohiko laughed at him mockingly.

"'Ha-ha-ha-ha! Do you see, Kyuta?! This is what you deserve! The winner is my father, Iozen! Understand?!'

"'You fool! How could this be excusable?!' Iozen shouted a stern rebuke at Ichirohiko.

"Kyuta was losing control of himself from the shock. His hair fluttered and stood on end. His hooded sweatshirt ballooned out, filled with an unnatural gust of air, and its front split open as the zipper pulled down. There on Kyuta's exposed chest was a swirling black hole. Exactly the same as Ichirohiko's…

"'No, Kyuta!' the grandmaster yelled sharply.

"But the words did not seem to reach the young man. The sword at his waist clattered and shook on its own, and some unseen force ripped apart the string that sealed it shut. Drawn from its scabbard, the sword floated in the air as if by telekinesis and turned its point toward Ichirohiko on the other side of the arena.

"'……?!'

"Ichirohiko looked at Kyuta in shock.

"'How dare you…!' Kyuta snarled in a low voice with unconcealed anger.

"'How dare you…!!'

"The point of the sword quivered, but nevertheless aimed accurately at Ichirohiko.

"'Kyuta! Resist the darkness!'

"The grandmaster shouted again in an effort to stop him.

"'Brother!'

"Jiromaru grabbed on to Ichirohiko's leg, as if to shield his brother from the sword with his own body.

"'Please stop, Kyuta! Aah, this is horrible!'

"Iozen could do nothing but hold his head in his hands miserably.

"Kyuta let the flames of his hatred flare up and trembled as he let out a roar:

"'Aaaaaaaaargggh!'

"Kyuta's sword instantly flew forward, like an arrow shot from a bow.

"It sliced though the air at tremendous speed toward Ichirohiko.

"That moment—

"'Squeak!'

"Poking out from under Kyuta's sweatshirt, Chiko raced quickly up Kyuta's head with clear resolve and bit Kyuta sharply on the nose.

"'Ack!'

"Kyuta spontaneously covered his face with his right hand from the pain.

"The red string tied around his wrist caught his eye.

"'…Kaede.'

"Kyuta snapped back to his senses.

"The hole in his chest shriveled rapidly.

"At the same time, Kyuta's sword, which had been rushing through the air, stopped short just in front of Ichirohiko's face. Losing the source of its power, the sword became inanimate once again and fell onto the arena floor.

"'*Kyu ta... Y ou... I w ill ne ver... for give...*'

"Ichirohiko was shuddering with hatred. The darkness at his chest grew and spread.

"The grandmaster whispered in dismay:

"'The darkness...it's consuming Ichirohiko.'

"Ichirohiko's body was now completely covered by the darkness.

"'... *Ne ver... for give yo u...*'

"Leaving behind that muffled voice, Ichirohiko's body instantly disappeared from the spot.

"When Jiromaru opened the eyes he had kept tightly shut, the brother he should have been clinging to was gone.

"'...Brother? Where are you? Brother?'

"He looked around in surprise, but his brother was nowhere to be seen.

"Unnoticed, the evening sun was streaming into the coliseum.

"Kyuta was panting from the absurd degree of exhaustion. Covered in sweat, he could barely stand. But he still forced his eyes to open in slits. He saw Kumatetsu with the sword stuck in his back. Still slumped over, Kumatetsu lay motionless.

"Kyuta muttered with his mind in a haze:

"'Hey... What are you...sleeping...for? Wake...up. Wake...'

"He got that far before losing consciousness and collapsing with a thud on the spot."

THE
DARKNESS

I could hear a voice in the darkness.

"…Kyuta. …Kyuta."

The voice drew gradually closer.

"Kyuta… Kyuta!"

I suddenly saw Kumatetsu before me. He was in the front yard of the hut with a giant cumulus cloud behind him, in his usual attire with his great sword slung over one shoulder. He was bellowing at me.

"Hurry up! Hurry, hurry, hurry! What're you doing, Kyuta?! Get your ass over here for training!"

Not so loud, jeez. Stop yelling.

Fine. I'm getting up now, so just wait a sec…

I awoke.

I found myself on some clean white sheets. Apparently, I had been sleeping with my face down on the edge of a bed.

I could see Chiko close by.

"Squeak. …Squeak, squeak!"

Chiko bounded up and down as if to greet to me.

"…Chiko."

I called out, half awake, half asleep.

"Squeak! Squee…"

Chiko continued chirping as if to tell me something.

"…What's up, Chiko?"

Where was I? It was a domed space, wide and brightly lit. I could see a wooden wall designed with what looked like geological formations. Hadn't I been at the coliseum? I'd watched Kumatetsu's match, Kumatetsu had won, then I'd high-fived him… And then…

I finally remembered.

Realizing what had happened, I sprang up.

On top of those white sheets lay Kumatetsu, on the verge of death.

"……!"

My heart heaved heavily. My head was numb, and I couldn't think.

Covered in bandages with an IV tube stuck in his arm, Kumatetsu was completely still. But a closer look revealed that his lips were moving slightly as he breathed softly. Next to his pillow was the crimson sheath covered in scratches.

How sad and distorted he had become. The Kumatetsu I knew wasn't like this at all. He was a ridiculously vigorous guy who yelled a lot, ate a lot, and laughed a lot. He was a guy you couldn't kill even if you tried. But the Kumatetsu before me was struggling just to breathe. I had never even imagined Kumatetsu like this.

The tears were welling up.

Damn it.

I hung my head and silently struggled to keep them from flowing.

Damn it.

How could this have happened…?

I bit down hard on my lower lip.

"…I'm sorry. Ichirohiko, I'm so sorry…," Iozen muttered with unbearable grief, sitting on a sofa with his head hung down weakly. Alongside him were Jiromaru and Jiromaru's mother.

The place was something like a living room in the grandmaster's hermitage, and the dome-shaped space had a huge circular skylight in it as big as a planetarium screen. The stars were starting to twinkle in the twilight sky visible through the skylight.

Illuminated by the gentle light of a lantern, the grandmaster spoke.

"That power Ichirohiko used certainly isn't the telekinesis that beasts use. It's clearly something borne of the darkness that humans alone harbor in their hearts."

"Grandmaster. Then you knew all along…?"

"Iozen, you shall tell us what happened."

"It was back when I was still young, when I was wandering around a human city on my own. The sound of a crying infant came flying into my ear. It was raining that afternoon, and the noise was immediately erased by the sound of raindrops and splashing. But when I spread out the hood of my cloak and carefully perked up my ears, I could definitely hear it: the faint cry of an infant, so feeble that it could stop at any moment. I gazed around at the passers-by, but the sound didn't seem to reach any of their human ears. Instantly realizing that I might have been the only one capable of responding to the cry, I pushed through the passing umbrellas and walked all over in search of the sound, listening as carefully as I could. Then finally I discovered the place where the voice was coming from. Deep among some multi-tenant build-ings, away from prying eyes, was a narrow space with a red umbrella, opened and propped up to one side. I moved the umbrella aside to find an infant about eight months old, wrapped in cloth and placed in a basket.

"I carefully picked the infant up in my arms. In the basket along with some toys and the infant's water bottle was a letter. Seeing that, I instinctively understood that the real parents must have done this under truly dire circumstances. In the human world with nobody to hear its infant cries, the child wouldn't have lasted. That being the case…I decided on the spot to bring the child back with me to Jutengai. In other words, I made up my mind to secretly raise the infant. Of course, I knew that humans can harbor darkness in their hearts, but I thought that as long as I raised him properly, as long as I gave him all of my love, he would be all right.

"Thinking back on it now, that was brash of me. It was a foolish assumption.

"As Ichirohiko grew, he questioned me repeatedly.

"'Father. Why does my nose not grow long like yours?'

"'Fear not. Soon enough, it will start growing.'

"'Why have I not grown tusks like Jiromaru and yourself?'

"'Do not worry. The time will come.'

"'Father, what am I, exactly…?'

"'Ichirohiko, you are my son. You are son to Iozen and nothing else.'

"I could not find anything else to tell him."

"The more you tried to convince him that he was the child of a beast, the more Ichirohiko lost faith in himself and deepened the darkness within him."

The grandmaster let out a sigh. "Who would have thought the air in the beast world would expose a hole in a human's chest so…?"

Peeking in from outside of the door, I pressed my hand against my own chest.

Then I heard Jiromaru speak up quietly.

"What do you mean, 'darkness'? I'm too stupid to understand. I don't care who my brother really is. To me, my brother's my brother."

So saying, Jiromaru looked at his mother and father with a face full of naïve compassion. Jiromaru's mother's eyes brimmed with tears. Iozen looked up beseechingly.

"Grandmaster. Must we give up hopes of living with Ichirohiko again? …Is it too late for us to start over…?"

He expressed the only wish that mattered almost as if to himself, in a voice so soft it threatened to disappear.

I felt my chest seize up as I listened.

The grandmaster turned a stern face toward Iozen.

"Even now, Ichirohiko is adrift somewhere. Unless we can drive the darkness out of him, nothing else can be done."

I'm the only one who can do something about Ichirohiko.
Unbeknownst to anyone, I made up my mind.

"From there, Kyuta prepared to set off.

"He quickly checked the state of his sword, then put it into its bag and slung it over his back. He then slipped out of the grandmaster's hermitage and made his way down the garden steps that led to the exit.

"I called out after his departing back:

"'Hey, Kyuta.'

"Kyuta stopped and slowly turned around.

"'How could you leave Kumatetsu behind like this…?' I asked in a bereft voice. Where was he going, with Kumatetsu in such a state? I wanted Kyuta to stay beside the guy.

"But Kyuta said nothing and only stared back up at me, and I didn't know what more to say.

"Then suddenly, Hyakushubo yelled at Kyuta from beside me in a booming voice:

"'Idiot! Is it revenge you seek?! What good will that do?!'

"This took me completely by surprise, and I looked at Hyakushubo standing next to me with his arms crossed. Even though I've known Hyakushubo for ages, this was the first I'd ever seen him like this. He was always calm and had always been on Kyuta's side, but just in that moment, he stood there with his eyes narrowed, scolding Kyuta in a deep tone I had never heard him use before.

"'I've had enough. If you think I'll always be soft on you, you've got another think coming! Have you learned nothing from seeing Kumatetsu the way he is, you fool?!'

"I then looked at Kyuta, assuming he'd be startled and at a loss at Hyakushubo's sudden change in manner.

"But the kid just stared straight back at Hyakushubo with a steady resolve in his eyes. There was no uncertainty there whatsoever. They were the eyes of a man who had made up his mind.

"'Kyuta…!'

"Seeing this, Hyakushubo immediately undid his arms. With Kyuta looking at him like that, he had no choice but to accept Kyuta's decision. Hyakushubo returned to normal and simply asked Kyuta worriedly:

"'…But you're going anyway?'

"Kyuta simply nodded yes, just like he used to when he was a kid.

"'Thanks for scolding me. I feel upright and ready now.' I could tell he was trying to explain what he was thinking as carefully as possible. 'But you should know this isn't about revenge. Ichirohiko and I are the same, and I could have turned out like Ichirohiko if something had gone wrong. The only reason I didn't is thanks to all the people who raised me. That's you, Uncle Tata, and Uncle Hyaku, and everyone else…'

"His words astonished me.

"'Kyuta…you…'

"Then Kyuta put his hand to his own chest.

"'But I can't dismiss this as if it wasn't my concern at all. What Ichirohiko's dealing with is the same as what I'm dealing with, so…I'm going. …Please take good care of him.'

"How could we refuse when he put it like that? But then on top of that, he went and bowed his head down low. Suddenly, I was overwhelmed with love for the boy. I ran down the stone steps and grabbed Kyuta's neck to pull him into a hug.

"'Okay! I hear your determination loud and clear! Leave Kumatetsu to us. We'll keep a good eye on him. So go. Go on!'

"As I slapped Kyuta on the back over and over again, I couldn't stop crying.

"I've gotta tell you, this was completely out of character for me. But I started thinking about how Kyuta had grown to be so reliable, and the tears just started pouring out."

*   *   *

"After we saw Kyuta off, Tatara and I headed for the infirmary in the grandmaster's hermitage so that we could stay by Kumatetsu's side, just as Kyuta had asked us to. Kumatetsu was covered in bandages, still lying down. The two of us leaned against the wall and watched the side of Kumatetsu's face in a daze.

"No, it wasn't actually Kumatetsu that we were looking at.

"Through our eyes, we could see Kyuta back when he was still a little boy.

" 'Thanks to all the people who raised me,' he said...'

"I repeated what Kyuta had said earlier out loud.

"Beside me, Tatara blinked contemplatively.

" 'Who would've thought that'd mean us, too?'

" 'Well, we *have* always been around since Kyuta was little.'

" 'Yeah. He was such a cheeky, annoying little brat at first.'

" 'We went over every day, through wind or rain.'

" 'We'd look after him, but he wouldn't look the least bit thankful.'

" 'But then suddenly, before we even realized, he's all grown-up.'

" 'And he's talking like a man.'

" '...How proud he makes us.'

" 'So proud...'

"Just then—

" '...Urgh...'

"A low groan snapped us back to the present.

" '...Kumatetsu!'

"Kumatetsu had regained consciousness."

I made my way through the complicated, tangled alleyways of Jutengai and emerged in Shibuya at night.

The huge screen of the QFRONT building wavered in the awful humidity. Noisy music from all around intermingled and reverberated. The footsteps from the many people who filled the hectic intersection made the ground tremble.

Swaying in the wind all over Center Gai were leaved bamboo branches with colorful strips of paper and streamers—decorations for the star festival. It was the first weekend of summer break, and I could see countless young people walking around in groups. Everyone looked so happy, so oblivious, so carefree. Here was the "normal" life that I had once longed for, I thought. And there I stood, the only one there for reasons that weren't "normal."

I called Kaede's cell number from a pay phone.

I always let it ring once then hung up immediately. Then her phone would indicate that she had missed a call from a pay phone. I was pretty much the only one who contacted Kaede using a pay phone. Then I would wait near the station in a spot we had agreed on beforehand. Kaede might come if it was in the afternoon and still light out. She might have a prior engagement and show up late, or she might not be able to come at all. It didn't matter either way. I would just read a book and wait. That was how we always arranged to meet up.

But today was different. It was the first time I had contacted her at night.

After a while, Kaede showed up at our meeting spot. She said that she had slipped out of the house so that her parents wouldn't notice. She was wearing a white dress with navy stripes and sneakers. Hugging a shoulder bag under her arm, she looked at me with concern, out of breath.

I held out my copy of *The Whale*.

"I want you to keep this for me."

"…What? Why?"

I had told Kaede some things but not others, and certain things in particular were incredibly difficult to explain properly. But in that moment, I decided to be as honest as I could.

"I have someone I need to settle things with. I don't know if I'll be able to win. If I lose, that might be it for me. That's why."

"But…"

"I'm glad I met you, Kaede. I was able to learn so much I didn't know because of you. It really helped me see just how big the world is."

"What are you saying? This is only the beginning…"

"I was really happy that we got to study together, you know? So I just wanted to say thank you."

"Wait…I don't want this. Don't say that!"

Kaede shouted and shook her head in denial.

That was when I heard it.

"*Th ere y ou ar e.*"

I jerked my head around, sensing something horrible that made me shudder. Chiko squeaked sharply in warning.

"*W on't fo rgive yo u.*"

It was Ichirohiko. There he was, in the distance beyond the people crowding Center Gai, glaring sharply my way with crazed eyes. I instinctively readied myself to protect Kaede. I couldn't believe it. Had he come after me all this way?

"*Low ly hum an.*"

Shadowy darkness swirled on Ichirohiko's chest like a bottomless swamp. The pale blue glow emanating from his body seemed to indicate the intense power of his hatred.

But the pedestrians merely glanced at the glowing Ichirohiko and passed by as if nothing was wrong. Did they think it was a performance of some kind? None of them seemed to sense any danger.

I could see Ichirohiko step forward slowly with his eyes fixed on us.

"No… Not here…!"

"That's…your opponent…?" Kaede asked, realizing the situation.

"It's dangerous. Run. In the opposite direction from me," I whispered.

But Kaede moved to hold my hand. Her clammy, stiff fingers trembled in fear.

"What are you doing?!"

I pried my hand away and tried to push her off. "Go! Hurry!"

But Kaede shook her head violently and struggled to stay by me. Still trembling, she grabbed my hand even tighter.

"I'm not letting you go…!"

"……!"

I didn't know what to do. Meanwhile, Chiko emitted an even shriller squeak to alert us of the danger.

I could see Ichirohiko moving in our direction, eyes still fixed on us.

"…Damn it!"

Seeing no other choice, I pulled Kaede by the hand, pushing my way through the crowd and running down Center Gai toward the station.

Ichirohiko gradually picked up speed and came straight after us.

"Run as hard as you can!" I called out to Kaede as I pulled her along.

A heavy slamming noise came from behind and I turned back.

"?!"

Ichirohiko was running wild like a train out of control, viciously ramming into the people who just happened to be in his path and tossing them aside as if they were pebbles on the roadside. Abrupt screams erupted one after the other. People around were watching in a daze at the madness of the situation.

"…Damn!"

I had to run, but I couldn't let him wreak any more havoc, either. I needed to make a decision.

"Kaede! Stand back!"

I let go of Kaede's hand abruptly and went back the way we had come.

"Aah!"

This made Kaede topple onto the ground, but I couldn't deal with that just then. I faced Ichirohiko, wielding my sheathed sword, still in its bag.

"Yaaaaah!"

Meanwhile, Ichirohiko drew his sword from his waist with no hesitation. Its sharp blade gleamed menacingly.

"*A aa a a r!*"

The two swords collided fiercely with a bang.

I managed to meet Ichirohiko's strike from overhead, just barely. I could tell that the blade of Ichirohiko's sword had wedged itself deeply into the scabbard inside its bag.

As we crossed blades at the crossroads where the sign to the LoFt store could be seen on the right-hand side, the pedestrians watched with apprehensive curiosity.

"Huh? What's going on?"

"Are they shooting a TV show or something?"

I couldn't even spare a moment to tell them to hurry and run. Ichirohiko was pushing me back with unnatural strength. It was all I could do to hold him back. The swords grated abrasively against each other.

"Damn...!"

Overpowered, I had no choice but to give ground. I had to pull my sword back, but Ichirohiko seized the chance to swipe his blade sideways at me. I instinctively ducked and just barely dodged it. But a second strike on the return grazed my face as I leaped backward. I could tell that my left cheek had been cut. The cut was maybe three centimeters long. The sword had only lightly grazed me, but it had cut through my skin like paper. There was still no blood.

"*A a a aa r!*"

Ichirohiko roared and swung his sword down from overhead. I held up my weapon sideways and caught it just in time. Blood seeped out of the cut on my left cheek. As he pressed down with all his strength as if to snap the blade with its scabbard in two, Ichirohiko's eyes widened madly.

In that moment, I felt the fear of death right before me, for the first time in my life. This wasn't a match safeguarded by rules. My opponent was Ichirohiko—but not Ichirohiko, at the same time. He was trying to kill me in his crazed state. My own eyes went wide. I couldn't afford to hold back any longer. If I didn't go at him with all my might without letting my guard down for an instant, I was a goner.

"...Raaaar!"

I pushed against Ichirohiko frantically. Ichirohiko staggered backward, and that force made his sword fall onto the Center Gai tiles with a dry clattering sound. In a flash, I swung my sword in its bag up high and smashed it down on Ichirohiko with all the strength I could muster.

"Yaaaaaaaaaaaah!"

A dull thud echoed around. I had aimed diagonally for the shoulder, but he blocked the strike at the last moment with his left forearm. Still, a direct hit was a direct hit. The blow should have been enough to break bone.

However...

"?!"

I could hardly believe my eyes. Ichirohiko's left arm had somehow bulged out as big as an elephant's and was blocking the sword.

"*Kyu ta...*"

Ichirohiko lifted his downcast face. At the same time, the hat with the boar's face slipped down, obscuring the top half of his face. The inanimate boar's face glared at me with its button eyes and sewn-on nose and tusks. I recoiled for a moment at the sheer horror of it. The hole in his chest spread with a low hum.

The next moment, Ichirohiko held up his right hand, which bulged into a colossal fist as large as he was tall and struck me with incredible force. I put up my guard without understanding what had happened and was thrown several dozen meters away. If I had simply slammed into the wall of a building, perhaps that would have been it for me. But fortunately just before that happened, my entire body plunged into a star-festival decoration that had been tied up arch-like over Center Gai, and the intertwined bamboo branches flexed heavily, cushioning the impact. I flipped over on the spot and fell, bouncing off the awning of the camera shop directly below before slamming onto the tiles on the ground.

"Agh!"

The pain was so intense that I couldn't breathe. Kaede rushed over as I groaned, huddling on the ground.

"Ren!"

Sharp screams burst out from around us. The onlooking pedestrians must have finally caught on to how dangerous Ichirohiko might be. They started running this way and that in a panic.

Ichirohiko stood there amid the uproar with his hat still over his eyes, grinning creepily with just the lower half of his face. The button eyes sewn on flashed coldly. As the hole in his chest grew bigger, the glow from his body strengthened all the more.

"Oh no…"

I heard Kaede whisper, horrified.

I knew Ichirohiko would keep coming after me, no matter what. No matter what kind of unimaginable form he morphed into, he wasn't going to stop chasing me.

I stood up with Kaede's support and escaped into an alleyway, dragging a leg.

"Damn it. I can't fight here. I need to find someplace…"

But where in the middle of Shibuya could there be a place that wouldn't endanger anyone else?

—Ichirohiko picked up a thick book that had been left out on the road. It was the copy of *The Whale* that Kaede had dropped when she had fallen over.

"… Wh al e…?"

So muttering, he began to transform himself—.

Coming out of Center Gai onto the main road, I shouted to everyone and anyone I saw.

"It's dangerous! Don't go that way! Hurry and run!" I hollered at every person I passed by. But nobody cared to listen. Just after eight o'clock, Shibuya was still overflowing with people and cars.

And then…

An eerie shadow came creeping under the feet of the people crossing the street at the bottom of Dogenzaka. That wasn't all. The shadow also slid creepily beneath the tires of the city buses and taxis lined up in the heavy traffic.

"Huh?"

"What's this?"

"What's that shadow?"

The people stopped and squinted at their feet, but they couldn't tell anything. They couldn't even gauge just how big the thing was, much less comprehend what was casting it. Next, an odd sound that tapered off gradually, like the cry of an animal, echoed throughout the city. The people looked around in search of its source. It seemed as though it was coming from the shadow beneath their feet. A closer look revealed that the shadow was apparently moving slowly in one direction.

The immense shadow, wide enough to fill the road with three lanes on either side, drifted lazily into the intersection, then stopped with obvious purpose. Only the people looking down from the surrounding buildings could see it in its entirety. The shape of the shadow was almost like…

"A whale…"

Everyone gazed at the enormous shade swimming through Shibuya as if it were a dream.

"?!"

Beneath the elevated JR train tracks, Kaede and I looked back at the intersection. We sensed that the enormous shadow had discovered where we were. Danger was imminent. I yelled as loudly as I could at the drivers in the trailer trucks and cars underneath the tracks.

"Get out of your vehicles and run! Just do it!"

Suddenly, the ground in the intersection surged heavily, and the shadow rose up. It was as if a whale had poked its back through the water's surface.

The next moment, a heavy-duty trailer truck that had been sitting on the road heaved forward as if pushed by a strong force from behind, crashing into the row of cars stopped in front of it. There was commotion all around. The drivers hastily abandoned their vehicles and just barely escaped. The trailer truck rammed through the empty cars one by one and closed in on Kaede and I.

"Run!"

We followed the drivers and ran under the elevated tracks.

Then Kaede suddenly tripped on something and fell. "Oh!"

Just then, the trailer truck was forced onto the other vehicles and slammed straight into the side of the JR overpass, letting out a deafening crash.

I heard a scream from behind me.

"Kaede!"

I rushed back, helping Kaede up as a ton of rubble fell around us, and fled with all my might. The steel frame of the overpass groaned, contorted, and let out an odd, ear-splitting shriek like the cry of a monster.

Kaede and I turned back when we got to the Miyamasuzaka-shita intersection. Numerous cars were crushed on top of one another under the tracks, spewing white smoke. But the next moment, the sound of a huge explosion rang out, and the tracks were engulfed in a giant flame.

"......!"

The explosion was due to some leaked gasoline. If it had ignited just a little sooner, we might have been caught in those flames. No, it wasn't just us. Innocent bystanders could have been harmed.

"...How do I beat him...?"

Lit by the roaring flames, I looked on in dismay. Ichirohiko was no longer an opponent I could hope to take on with a sword. Then what could I possibly do...? Losing confidence, I had half given up.

But Kaede seemed to think of something and firmly pulled my hand with a resolute look.

"Ren, this way!"

"Where are we going?!"

"Just come!"

Kaede led me through the crossing in the intersection and ran quickly down the steps of the number twelve exit leading down into the Shibuya subway station. The shadow of the whale—Ichirohiko—didn't notice that we had gone underground and was left to wander around Aoyama Dori Street. Kaede's judgment on the spur of the moment had saved us.

The explosion on the JR overpass had thrown Shibuya Station into chaos.

Having run down the stairs from the number twelve exit into Shibuya Station, we saw the electronic boards above the turnstiles to the Yamanote, Saikyo, and Rinkai lines announce that those lines were all currently stopped due to fire. Immediately, the electronic boards for the Ginza Line, as well as the Hanzomon and Denentoshi lines, also displayed that operations were stalled, one after the other. It would only be a matter of time before a crowd of people unable to take the trains would flood the entire station.

Kaede swiftly ran down the mazelike steps in the station, leading me by the hand. She predicted that the line located in the deepest level of the station might still be unaffected by the chaos on the surface.

Kaede's guess was spot on.

The Fukutoshin Line alone was still operating.

Scheduled to leave Shibuya at 20:40, the Fukutoshin Line train bound for Shinjuku-sanchome was mostly empty.

Due to the darkness of the tunnel, I could see myself reflected dimly in the glass window of the carriage.

What can I do to fight him?

As the train rocked me in my seat, I interrogated my reflection in the glass.

The only weapon I have is a sword. But a sword's not enough to take him on with anymore. I'll just have to use it in a different way. Maybe if I open up the hole in my chest and trap all of his darkness inside, I can thrust the sword into myself and disappear from this world along with him…

I questioned the me reflected in the glass.

Is that all that's left for me to do now?

My reflection offered no reply.

But then—

"You know, I've been wondering…"

Next to me, Kaede spoke softly as if remembering something. "Why am I running with you, holding your hand? I'm scared beyond belief, but I'm still here, and I was wondering why."

"……?"

"I remember now. When I first met you, Ren, and we started

studying together, it made me really happy. I mean, I've never seen any-one enjoy studying as much as you. When I was with you, it gave me the courage to try harder myself."

"……"

"So it's no different now. If you're fighting, Ren, I'm with you."

Kaede looked at me with eyes full of conviction. "Don't forget. We never actually fight alone, ever."

"…Kaede."

The train slid into the station, and it became bright outside the window. My reflection in the glass disappeared into the light.

We never actually fight alone.

I repeated those words inside my mind.

The onboard monitor indicated that we had arrived at "Meiji-jingumae (Harajuku)." We heard an announcement from the driver.

"Attention, passengers. Due to a fire that occurred at Shibuya Station, the Fukutoshin Line will stop until further notice. Therefore, this station will be the last stop for this train. I repeat…"

As it turned out, we were unable to get out of Shibuya City.

THE SWORD
IN YOUR HEART

"At the very same time, Jutengai was in an uproar.

"The bridge next to the square had suddenly fallen apart as if it had exploded, emitting trails of white smoke. This was followed by numerous tremors concentrated on the main east hill road that shook the ground all over the city. These were clearly different from what we knew as normal earthquakes, and the shocks felt as if they had been caused by some giant, invisible thing thrashing violently about. The beasts were all stunned and alarmed by this mysterious phenomenon, and the square and night market stalls that were usually noisy and bustling in the evenings were heavy with an air of indescribable fear and confusion.

"Beasts yearning for an explanation flocked to the grandmaster's hermitage, and the grandmaster opened up the circular hall for them.

"The hall was ordinarily used by the city council, where the grandmaster led them to discuss and settle various issues. Meticulously polished wooden panels lined the wall of the circular space, illuminated by spotlights from above. The numerous lights crowding the ceiling and the aged pine trees painted all along the walls, like noh theater backdrops, were remnants from back when the hall had been used as a theater. The space was normally closed off to the general public.

"But this was an emergency. The hall was filled with nervous-looking beasts.

"With a resounding bang, a great shudder rocked the ground.

"The councillors, with cloth draped over their shoulders, all spoke up at once.

"'What is this tremor?'

"'Ichirohiko is raging about in the human world, trying to get at Kyuta.'

"'I realize that our world and the human world resonate with each other, but to think the effects would be this pronounced…'

"'Grandmaster, what is to become of Jutengai?'

"The councillors all looked to the grandmaster with concern.

"'Hmm…'

"The grandmaster closed his eyes and did not answer them.

"The councillors exchanged glances and talked among themselves.

"'Why should we be dragged into a fight between humans?'

"'It was a mistake to bring humans into our world in the first place.'

"Suddenly, the beasts off in a corner of the hall broke out in a commotion. The councillors all turned with questioning looks. The grandmaster looked up as well. The beasts opened up a path, and there—

"'……?'

"There came Kumatetsu lurching along on unsteady feet, using his great sword as a cane to support himself.

"Panting heavily, Kumatetsu stopped and lifted his face full of greasy sweat. The beasts around him all gasped at the tragic sight of his heavily bandaged body.

"Tatara and I got to the hall a moment later, rushing to catch up and hold Kumatetsu back.

"'Kumatetsu! Don't push things, or you'll die!'

"'You're in no state to be moving around!'

"'Shaddup!'

"Kumatetsu forced us off and attempted to step forward. 'Yo, Grandmaster… I heard what's going on. Let me take care of this… Let me…'

"'Kumatetsu…'

"'What the hell do you think you can do?!' Tatara cried out in a shrill scream. But no matter what he said, Kumatetsu wasn't one to listen. It had always been that way. All we could do was look on from behind.

"Kumatetsu edged forward using his weapon as support.

"'Grandmaster, you're the only one... The only one who can do something about this... But you're choosing to keep it to yourself.'

"'There's a way?'

"The councillors all cocked their heads. The beasts who were there looked at one another.

"'What does Kumatetsu mean for him to do?'

"'......'

"Still the grandmaster kept his eyes closed and said nothing.

"Straining under the pain from his injuries and with little time to spare, Kumatetsu was short of breath and seemed to be just barely standing on his feet. Yet his eyes alone had a sharp gleam to them, as if he was ready to take on another fight.

"'Kyuta may think he's all grown-up, but he needs someone to help him... I may be an outcast and an idiot, but I'm going to be of use to him all the same. I'm going to fill what he's missing in his heart... That there... That's the one thing an outcast like me can do!'

"Another tremor rocked the hall with an echoing bang.

"The grandmaster broke his silence and let out a sigh.

"'...Hm. To think the day would come for you to say something like that.'

"He then slowly surveyed everyone in the hall and spoke. 'He's asking me to hand over my privilege to reincarnate, you see.'

"The councillors all stared at Kumatetsu in shock.

"'You mean to reincarnate into a god?!'

"'Impossible! Not just any beast can do that!'

"'Unless, say, you were to be grandmaster, that isn't...'

"'Oh...?!'

"All of the beasts present came to a sudden realization.

"'But...'

"'Kumatetsu *is* grandmaster now.'

"The beasts all glared at Kumatetsu with understanding.

"The grandmaster walked toward the wheezing Kumatetsu.

"'Listen well, Kumatetsu. Once you decide to become a god, there is no going back. Is that understood?'

"Kumatetsu lifted his face slowly and looked squarely at the grandmaster.

"The grandmaster saw Kumatetsu's resolve in that stare.

"'…What am I to do with you? There's not a smidgen of doubt in your eyes…'"

Kaede and I got off the subway and emerged from underground.

Omotesando was seriously congested. The disaster that had occurred at Shibuya Station was having an effect here as well. We waded through the sea of people and went up the slope toward Harajuku Station. Kaede said that the only place nearby with relatively few people around was Yoyogi Park, or if not that, the Yoyogi National Gymnasium. In particular, although the stone paved bridge of the gymnasium was commonly used as a shortcut from Yoyogi toward Shibuya, Kaede assumed that the place would empty out once the gates were closed. We might be able to hide ourselves there, or even if we were found, we were likely to avoid putting other people in harm's way.

We entered the Yoyogi National Gymnasium's grounds before the gates closed at nine. There were no events happening there that day, and the gymnasium wasn't even lit up. We ran across the stone paved bridge beside the Yoyogi First Gymnasium and paused to rest once we got to the southeast wall.

I looked up at the unique silhouette of the First Gymnasium once again. Two main pillars towered high above in the darkness. The wires stretching down like a rope bridge from the pillars were also enormous. I felt like the building had a special presence that set it apart from any

of the architecture around it. I remembered hearing that it had originally been constructed to host the swimming events during the 1964
Tokyo Olympics. This location was where the coliseum stood in Jutengai. Only a few hours ago, Kumatetsu and Iozen had been fighting
there…

I was letting my mind wander when—

"Ren!" Kaede yelled sharply.

Way off in the distance, on the sidewalk we had been running on,
Ichirohiko appeared, seeming to emerge from nothing.

I hastily braced myself. He must have found us somehow and had
been following us all this time.

As soon as I blinked, though, Ichirohiko had disappeared into the
dark of the night, leaving behind the sound of a sharp swish.

"…He disappeared?"

I concentrated my attention left and right, making sure to guard
Kaede.

But it was under our feet that the transformation occurred. The
paved stones glowed with a diffused reflection that wavered as if we were
peering underwater. At the same time, the ground trembled slightly
with a low rumble. The tremors seemed to be getting bigger. It felt as if
something colossal was headed our way. What was going on…?

The next moment, that colossal something *leaped up* with an explosive boom.

What emerged was an immense sperm whale, large enough to fill
our entire field of vision.

"What…?!"

Kaede and I gazed up at the sky in dismay. Cloaked in a million tiny
particles of light and glowing a pale blue, the whale was exactly like the
Moby-Dick that appeared in *The Whale*. The only difference was the huge
tusks that protruded upward from its lower jaw, like those of a boar.

"Ichirohiko…!"

The glowing whale flipped its giant body around and closed in as if
to crash down on us. I pulled Kaede by the hand and ran. A split second

later, the glowing whale "splashed" directly into the paved stones, and a great burst of glowing particles surged up like water droplets, making the ground shudder tremendously.

Kaede couldn't help but let out a scream. We ran away frantically from the east edge of the bridge toward the Second Gymnasium. But the glowing whale shot up once again from under the pavement, blocking our way.

"?!"

A mass of glowing particles flooded the bridge. The whale then turned its back on the ground and slowly drifted through the sky. High above even the pillars of the First Gymnasium, it scowled down at the trivial specks that were us, as if to make it clear that there was nowhere to run.

A colossal whale drifting in the sky above Shibuya—such a supernatural sight was more than enough to put me in a stupor. What could I possibly do with just a tiny sword against something as overwhelming as this? I kept my eyes on the sky above and spoke to Kaede.

"Run, Kaede. He's after me."

"……!"

But instead of running, Kaede stepped forward.

"…Kaede?!"

Kaede headed for the spot directly below the whale, as if to challenge it.

"What is it that you want to do? Do you want to tear your hateful opponent to shreds? If you trample him and force him down, will you be satisfied?"

Kaede eyed the whale with a strong, unwavering gaze. That gaze pierced the eyes of the glowing whale.

"You may look like that now, but you're nothing more than human darkness bent on revenge!"

A crazed look flashed in the whale's—Ichirohiko's—eyes.

The whale stopped drifting and started descending toward Kaede.

"Everyone's equal when it comes to harboring darkness. Ren has it. I do, too!"

Kaede was trembling, yet she spoke as if to give herself courage. "...I'm still struggling the best I can to deal with what I have inside, too."

Sharp teeth lined the whale's lower jaw. It revealed glimpses of the solid black darkness deep inside its mouth, threatening Kaede. It urged her to give up, exposing an abyss so deep that, once inside, there was no getting out.

But Kaede firmly repulsed these threats.

"So against someone like you, who so easily gave in to darkness, there's no way Ren's going to lose..."

She slammed the only weapon she had—her strong will—against the whale with a cry.

"There's no way *we're* going to lose!"

The black abyss deep inside the whale's mouth threatened to swallow Kaede. At the last second, I grabbed her by the shoulders and leaped backward with all my might.

We were flung aside like tiny pebbles by the violent impact of the whale submerging. I protected Kaede with both of my arms as I soared through the air, rolling violently as I was dashed against the pavement again and again.

I made sure Kaede was all right, then ducked down and went for the whale on my own.

"Ren!"

Kaede's voice echoed from behind in an attempt to stop me. But I couldn't expose her to any more danger. I had no other choice left. I had to do it. There was no time to spare. I had to try the strategy I had come up with on the subway.

What had to be done, had to be done.

I pulled my sword out from its bag and stopped.

"Ichirohiko, look!" I shouted, immediately letting the hole in my chest open up.

As if drawn to the hole, Ichirohiko appeared on the pavement with a swish, followed by a splash of glowing particles that erupted from the ground before me. From within the splash emerged just the whale's head, as if it was spyhopping on the surface of water.

I raised my sword up high and loosened the blade from the scabbard above my head.

"I'll take all of your darkness inside myself!"

As the whale drew closer, the particles of light were swept up by a gust of wind.

"*Squeak!*"

Chiko came out of my collar and tried to stop me like before. But the tiny body was helplessly blown away by the heavy torrent of particles. If Kaede, stepping forward, hadn't made the catch with her hands, Chiko might have been lost somewhere.

Kaede realized something with a start. "Ren...you're not...?!"

The whale came closer, as if drawn to the hole in my chest. I drew the sword held over my head out in one swift motion. As soon as I absorbed him into my chest, I would plunge that sword into it.

"Come and disappear along with me!"

I could hear Kaede shouting frantically beyond the swirling blast of air.

"Ren! Don't give in!"

Then I heard something else.

"Kyuta!"

Someone called my name out loud and clear, and I snapped my head up.

A point up in the heavens glimmered for a moment, then "something" fell toward me at incredible speed.

It tore through the space between the whale and me, piercing the ground with a sharp thud and a violent tremor.

The next moment—

The whale let out a terrible scream, recoiling as if overwhelmed by the intense light of the flames emitted by that "something."

I was completely at a loss as to what had just happened.

But I had no trouble telling what that thing was sticking out of the ground before me; it was as long as I was tall.

It was Kumatetsu's great sword.

"Isn't this…his…?"

Still in its scabbard, it was glowing with intense light and wrapped in vicious flames.

But what was Kumatetsu's sword doing here…?

"Kyuta! That's Kumatetsu!"

"He reincarnated into a *tsukumogami*—the god of that blade."

It was Uncle Tata and Uncle Hyaku. They had suddenly appeared on top of the Yoyogi National Gymnasium and were looking down at me.

It took me a moment to comprehend what the two of them were talking about.

Tsukumogami? Reincarnated? Then…

"Then this is…him…?"

But why had Kumatetsu turned into a sword…?

"He said he was going to be the sword in your heart."

"The sword in my heart…?"

The sword, scratched all over its hilt and scabbard and battered from years of use, emerged from the pavement and floated into the air of its own accord. It then pointed its hilt toward my chest. Glowing and burning intensely, it slowly pushed itself in as if to fill the hole there.

Did he mean to fill what he could of my empty chest with that sword? Did he mean for those flames to illuminate the darkness that they say only humans harbor in their hearts?

Just then, I saw the image of Kumatetsu from bygone days superimposed over what I saw before me.

"You have one, right? A sword in your heart?!"

"Huh? Why would I?"

"The sword in your heart is what's important! Here! Right here!!"

I remembered it clearly.

Kumatetsu had beaten his chest over and over again, anxiously trying to get the nine-year-old me to understand. But at the time, I had just turned away and refused to even listen.

"Hey, now! You really came, eh? Yep, just like I figured. I'm impressed, kid!"

I clearly remembered Kumatetsu thumping over through those stalls at night, drinking gourd in hand, with a grin that filled his entire face. That was the first time he ever called me his apprentice.

"Nine…? Heh. Then from here on out, you're 'Kyuta.'"

I remembered Kumatetsu grinning happily, leaning against the sofa in that shamelessly cluttered hut as if it were yesterday. That was the moment I had become "Kyuta."

"Right, Kyuta! I'm gonna train you good, so you better be prepared!"

Then Kumatetsu had laughed, even though he was hurt all over from being pounded to a pulp by Iozen. At the time, I hadn't understood what he found funny at all.

But now I did.

Kumatetsu had just been happy, I was sure.

With the sword resting within, the hole in my chest closed up. I felt a tingling warmth throughout my chest.

The face of Kumatetsu laughing boisterously slowly faded from my mind.

If he was reincarnated, did it mean that I would never see him again? That we would never train together? Or eat together? At that thought, I got a choking feeling in my chest. Drops of tears welled up in my eyes and fell one by one. They just kept coming. I hugged my chest where Kumatetsu had disappeared.

But then—

"Kyuta!"

I suddenly heard that gruff voice I knew so well.

"What're you crying for, blockhead?!"

Huh? Where is that coming from?

"I hate hearing wusses cry!"

It was my chest.

The voice was echoing from inside my chest.

Kumatetsu—.

I was so startled that I couldn't find anything to say for a while.

But then I shook my head violently, whipping away the tears, and yelled with all of my might at my chest. "Shut up! I'm not crying!"

I snapped my head up to find the whale right in front of me. It was coming at me again, but just before it reached me, I saw my chest glow with a brilliant golden light. With a deafening electrifying crack, some powerful force repelled the whale.

From within my chest, Kumatetsu had repulsed the darkness using his newfound powers.

"? ? ? ?"

Ichirohiko, no longer in his whale form, was flung far away. He seemed confused, not comprehending what had just happened.

I picked up my own sword and put it back in its scabbard for the time being.

"We're settling this! Concentrate your energy!" Kumatetsu bellowed from within my chest.

Uncle Tata and Uncle Hyaku were watching over our fight.

"Kyuta..."

So was Kaede, and Chiko, too.

"Ren…"

Ichirohiko disappeared for a moment, and the whale leaped up once again from that spot. With an enormous reverberating crash, a mass of glowing particles splashed up. The whale sprung high into the sky over Shibuya with maddened rage, threatening us.

"Not yet! Sharpen your senses even more!"

I thrust the sword in my hand in front of me, waiting for the right moment.

With yet another crash, the whale threw its colossal body high once more.

Every time it emerged from the ground, it drew closer. It would leap up into the air, as if waiting for me to run away in fright.

Then I noticed something.

…What is that…?

I could see glimpses of Ichirohiko's figure beyond the splashes of glowing particles.

Ichirohiko always shows himself just before the whale emerges. If so…

Once I was sure, I gripped the hilt with my right hand, placed the sword against my waist, and dropped my body low. It was the stance for the quick-draw technique that I had learned from Kumatetsu.

"Find that one vital point! Then steady your aim and strike without hesitation!"

Kumatetsu's voice echoed within my chest.

I concentrated hard to determine exactly where and when it would emerge.

A resounding crash.

Wait for it.

Another crash.

Wait…

Then I chose a certain moment.

Now!

At almost the exact second, a gruff voice came from my chest:

"Now! Let 'er rip!"

I kicked the ground with all of my might and leaped up.

"Yaaaaah!"

I zoomed with ferocious speed through a space saturated with particles of light as far as the eye could see.

I used my thumb to push the sword out of its scabbard. The blade emitted a brilliant light as it slowly emerged.

I could feel Kumatetsu's great sword inside my chest also gradually reveal its own naked blade. Crimson flames spewed from the weapon.

Ichirohiko appeared ahead in my path.

"?!"

The boar's face that covered Ichirohiko's own seemed to wince and shudder as I closed in.

Spot on.

I took aim at my target.

"Aaaaah!"

Then I drew my sword from its scabbard with an explosive speed I had never experienced before.

Kumatetsu also drew his sword.

A flash of cold steel.

The two swords slashed through the darkness.

I quickly slid to a stop, my sword still extended at the end of its swing.

Struck by the swords, Ichirohiko hovered in a daze.

A moment later, the glowing whale leaped into the air above Yoyogi's First Gymnasium. More particles than ever before scattered about like a raging volcanic eruption.

Writhing in agony in the air, the tusked whale flickered erratically. A spine-chilling scream of a roar shook the roof of the gymnasium.

AAAAAaaar...

The dissonant, trailing howl reached its last crescendo like a death cry, then gradually grew weak and faint. The colossal body never submerged again, but seeped into the night sky above Shibuya, melting away. The very last of the seemingly infinite scatter of particles disappeared, and silence returned to the city as if nothing had ever happened.

"…Did they get him?" Uncle Tata asked in a strangled voice, watching from the roof of the gymnasium. Uncle Hyaku remained nervous as he peered down.

"No…"

I stood up and breathed in deeply, then put my sword back in its scabbard.

Turning around, I found Ichirohiko lying on the pavement unconscious.

"*Low ly hum an…*"

I looked at Ichirohiko's face as he continued to sleep.

Looking at his pale skin, thin arms, and long eyelashes, I could hardly believe that this was the opponent I had just had a fierce, deadly sword fight against.

Ichirohiko had agonized over who he was. Was he a beast, or was he a human? He had longed to become a beast but couldn't and detested humans though he was one himself. The conflict had thrown his mind into uncontrolled turmoil.

We're not beasts. We can never hope to become such beautiful beings. We are but fragile humans, cursing ourselves and struggling with the darkness in our hearts.

But if one thing was certain, it was that although we were both human, we lived among the beasts and were raised by them.

In other words, we were sons of beasts.

That was something I was truly proud of in that moment.

"Tatara and I lifted up the unconscious Ichirohiko and took him back to Jutengai. He was taken in by the grandmaster's hermitage for the time being to rest. Later on, the grandmaster would discuss what would become of him with the city council.

"Ichirohiko slept in a bedroom that was set up for him in the hermitage. As dawn approached, it started to grow light outside the window.

"Eventually, Ichirohiko opened his eyes like a blossoming flower.

"'......? ...Where am I?'

"Ichirohiko sat up in the large bed surrounded by a lace canopy. He found himself in silk pajamas of pure white. There was a wall designed with what looked like geological formations. White sheets. The smell of flowers. The fragrance of soap. Ichirohiko couldn't hide his confusion at finding himself in this unknown place.

"Then he noticed his family with their heads down on the foot of the bed, asleep.

"'Father, Mother...Jiromaru...'

"They had sat with him the entire night and had fallen asleep on the spot. Still unaware of this, Ichirohiko muttered as if to himself:

"'What have I been doing...? I thought we all went to the coliseum together, and then...'

"He tried to recall what had happened after that, but try as he might, he could not.

"Then suddenly, he noticed something.

"Someone had tied a red string around his right wrist.

"Here was something he clearly remembered seeing before.

"'This is...Kyuta's...?'

"He looked at the string on his wrist with wonder.

"Of course, it had been Kyuta who had tied that on. Kaede had tied it on Kyuta before that. Apparently, she had done so with the wish that if Kyuta was ever worried about himself or felt trapped, he would see the string and remember to restrain himself. Kyuta wished the same thing for Ichirohiko. He had passed the baton that Kaede gave him over to Ichirohiko.

"It was getting bright outside. Dawn was at hand.

"Around the same time, Kyuta was sitting on a spot overlooking the entire city of Shibuya in the early morning.

"All alone, he held his hand to his chest.

"No, not alone—there were two of them, to be precise. He was having a private chat with the Kumatetsu inside his chest.

"'Look, Kyuta. Once I decide to do something, I don't change that for nothing.'

"'Heh. I know.'

"'If you're ever being wishy-washy, I'll beat you up from inside.'

"'Shut up. I'll never be unsure again.'

"'That's what I want to hear.'

"'You just stay there quietly and watch what I do.'

"'Fine. Show me what you've got.'

"Kumatetsu grinned and laughed through his teeth.

"Kyuta also chuckled softly.

"The two of them just sat there, laughing together.

"Kumatetsu had indeed reincarnated. He gave up his physical form to become a sword embedded inside Kyuta's heart. He had become a fine god that any beast would yearn to be. Yet the conversation between the two then revealed that nothing had changed from the old days.

"God or not, Kumatetsu was Kumatetsu.

"Kyuta knew that perfectly well.

"The new day's sun peeked out from between the high-rise buildings. Kyuta took his hand off his chest and stood up. The morning light illuminated Kyuta radiantly.

"His demeanor then was nothing like the Kyuta from before.

"Kyuta was no longer the same Kyuta.

"It seemed to me that he had grown to be very strong indeed, ever maturing and ever changing."

"By the way, guess how the human world responded to the things that went on that night? They showed the blackened railway overpass on that huge monitor in front of the station and reported it like this:

*   *   *

"'Last night, a heavy-duty trailer truck went out of control, causing an explosion in the center of Shibuya, Tokyo. Many were lightly injured such as from falling, but the accident miraculously produced no serious injuries, including any to the driver of the truck. Police are interrogating the driver and will continue their investigation. There are also numerous witnesses insisting that they saw a large shadow similar to that of a whale before the accident, but nothing could be found on surveillance footage, and what really happened remains a mystery...'

"That's what they said.

"I couldn't help but burst out laughing when I heard.

"Humans really are strange creatures, aren't they?

"They totally refuse to believe the things they see with their very own eyes, after all!"

EPILOGUE

"Paper confetti fluttered against a clear summer sky with not a single cloud to be seen.

"The crowd of beasts congregating in the square welcomed Kyuta back with a great cheer.

"Kyuta had successfully overcome the colossal whale that had caused the eerie tremors the night before, and the word had spread throughout Jutengai by the next morning. Cries praising Kyuta for saving the city erupted all around. The grandmaster especially commended the fact that Kyuta, a human, had subdued another human's (Ichirohiko's) darkness gone out of control—all the more impressive when Kyuta harbored that same darkness within himself. The city council unanimously decided that they would hold a celebration to honor Kyuta. The preparations had already been made. Actually, the decorations around the city, as well as the feast, had originally been prepared to commemorate the new grandmaster, so they simply decided to put those to new use.

"Having returned to Jutengai, Kyuta was quite taken aback when he was told that there would be a celebration that afternoon to honor him. But the grandmaster explained that the celebration had originally been meant for Kumatetsu, but now that he had been reincarnated, the preparations would go to waste, and that it was Kyuta's duty as apprentice to accept it on his behalf. Persuaded by the grandmaster's peculiar logic, Kyuta ended up paraded through the city. Reluctant as he was, he had to answer the cries of the beasts who were grateful to Kyuta for saving the city. Kyuta walked through the crowds of welcoming beasts, looking shy and flustered.

"Tatara and I watched with pride at the young man in all his glory, with his sword slung over his shoulder.

"I turned to the fresh-faced apprentices looking at Kyuta in awe.

"'Take a good, long look. Even that Kyuta was merely a feeble child at first,' I told them.

"Their eyes all shined hopefully with excitement.

"Tatara continued.

"'In other words, if you fresh-faced beasts are diligent with your daily training, you'll come into your own someday...'

"'Maybe.'

"'Yup, maybe.'

"We couldn't be certain, naturally.

"Their hopefulness interrupted, the apprentices looked at us dejectedly.

"But what we meant to say was, do your best and don't despair even if you become discouraged.

"Isn't that right, Tatara?"

"Yeah, that's about right.

"Oh, and up until the start of the celebration, the grandmaster and city council had been engrossed in a long discussion. This was none other than to decide what would become of Ichirohiko.

"Our common belief had always been that humans shouldn't be allowed into the beast world because the darkness they harbored would bring about disaster. Based on that convention, Ichirohiko should have been returned to the human world. But on the other hand, Kyuta had been raised for years in the beast world despite being a human, and had not only conquered the darkness within himself but had also fought Ichirohiko's. Kyuta was now a recognized member of Jutengai. The beast world's reasoning for rejecting humans no longer held water, given Kyuta's example.

"In the end, the city council agreed to let Ichirohiko start over as Iozen's son. For his misdeed of deceptively raising Ichirohiko as a beast, Iozen was charged with the responsibility of raising him again into a fine, upstanding adult. Word has it that Iozen promised a new start with tears running down his face.

"Having ended the meeting, the grandmaster came out onto the balcony to look down at Kyuta in the center of the square.

"The guest sages were already drunk, with celebratory glasses held in their hands.

" 'The city wasn't damaged too much.'

" 'And Ichirohiko and Iozen will start over again.'

" 'Everything worked out.'

" 'But alas...'

"The grandmaster let his head droop. 'I let my chance to ascend to godhood slip away, thanks to that Kumatetsu. It's back to being grandmaster for me,' he complained with a sigh.

" 'Now, now. Today is for celebrating Kyuta.'

"Just then, a murmur rang out from among the beasts in the square.

" '...Oh? Behold,' the grandmaster said, looking at the small figure in the center of the commotion.

" 'That girl, too, is among those who supported Kyuta.'

"By 'that girl,' he meant Kaede, wearing a sleeveless light blue shirt and a long white skirt.

" 'Kaede... What are you doing here?'

"Kyuta gaped at Kaede with surprise.

"Kaede smiled and walked toward Kyuta, laughing softly.

" 'I got invited.'

"To tell you the truth... Heh-heh. It was none other than me, good ol' Tatara, who invited Kaede to Jutengai. Kaede and I had both cheered Kyuta on at the Yoyogi National Gymnasium, hadn't we? So I figured she was a crucial guest who just had to be at any celebration honoring Kyuta.

"Kaede whipped out the copy of *The Whale* that she had hidden behind her back and held it out to Kyuta.

"'Here! I dropped it, and it took me a while to find it. Here, you can have it back.'

"Kyuta took it from her, smiling.

"'...Thanks.'

"Then Kaede followed by whipping out another document.

"'And this! An application for the Equivalency Exam. What do you think? Do you still want to take it?'

"She smiled cheerfully at him.

"Kyuta looked down, a little embarrassed, and scratched the back of his neck.

"He didn't answer immediately.

"'You have to decide for yourself, Ren.'

"Kaede waited for his response.

"What she meant was this: He had to decide for himself whether he was going to spend his life in Jutengai or in the human world.

"After a long pause, seemingly thinking over it carefully, Kyuta gave a short reply:

"'I'll take it.'

"'...Yes!'

"Kaede's eyes sparkled as she spread her arms out wide, then clasped Kyuta's hands in hers.

"'I thought you'd say that! Let's do our best together!'

"'Yeah.'

"Just then—

"'Here come the fireworks!'

"The voice of a fireworks craftsman echoed from beyond the crowd, and the beasts in the square all murmured in delight.

"Skyrockets shot up all at once from the top of the hill.

"Colorful rings of light spread across the clear evening sky.

"Kaede looked up at them with sparkling eyes.

"Kyuta also looked up with a radiant smile on his face.

"All of the beasts looked up with cheer in their hearts.

"With those fireworks to kick off the celebration, the festivities raged on deep into the night."

"Kyuta returned to the human world.

"Are you lads curious to know how he's doing now?

"Truth is, I snuck over once to check on him.

"Kyuta and his father were meeting up in the shopping street in the evening. Having come home from work, Kyuta's father spotted Kyuta in the crowd and raised his hand with a smile. Kyuta responded with a smirk and lifted both hands laden with grocery store bags. As they walked home to their apartment, I saw them talking and laughing happily as they pushed their bikes along. Once they got home, I saw them step out onto the balcony and take down the laundry together, which I found quite heartwarming.

"Kyuta had finally begun living with his father.

"I was relieved to be able to see that come to pass, and also filled with a great sense of satisfaction.

"These days, he seems to be busy studying for his university exams.

"Kaede is keeping good watch over Kyuta, and I'm sure that Kyuta's late mother is also watching from somewhere afar.

"'Squeak!'

"Actually...

"She may be watching over him from somewhere surprisingly close."

"That's the end of Kyuta's story as we know it.

"Whadd'ya all think? Are you happy now that you've heard what you came to hear? Well, that's just great. Then go and use what you've learned here for your sword training.

"What's that? You wanna ask one last thing?

"Whether Kyuta quit being a swordsman?"

"It's true Kyuta never again took up a sword after that."

"But if you ask me, he's still the strongest swordsman there ever was."

"Yes, he's the only swordsman with a sword called Kumatetsu inside his heart."

"However tough things may get, Kyuta's sure to pull through in the end."

"What kind of things do you suppose he will accomplish in the human world?"

"We can't wait to see what the kid does.

"...Wouldn't you lot agree?"